Gospel of the
SPARROW

BERNICE ROYSLAND

ISBN 978-1-0980-0556-6 (paperback)
ISBN 978-1-0980-0557-3 (digital)

Copyright © 2019 by Bernice Roysland

All rights reserved. No part of this publication may be reproduced, distributed, or transmitted in any form or by any means, including photocopying, recording, or other electronic or mechanical methods without the prior written permission of the publisher. For permission requests, solicit the publisher via the address below.

Christian Faith Publishing, Inc.
832 Park Avenue
Meadville, PA 16335
www.christianfaithpublishing.com

Printed in the United States of America

To Carol Leafblad for sharing her insight on the Southern culture.
To the memory of Jean Dahling, who embraced the
philosophy of the fable during her lifetime and whose
obituary reads, "Jean Dahling—One does what one can."
To the memory of Suzanne Tjornhom, who graciously shared some
of her remembrances of Nigeria's cultural and educational concepts.
To the memory of Dorwin and Loralee Hansen, who were
early readers of the novel and offered much encouragement.

THE FABLE

The Arabian version of the fable "The Sky Is Falling" describes a sparrow lying in the middle of the road, feet up. When questioned by a passing horseman the little bird replies he has heard that the sky is falling, and he is holding it up. Laughing, the horseman asks the sparrow if he thinks he can hold up the whole sky by himself. The sparrow stretches its tiny legs and replies, "One does what one can."

Chapter 1

BEGINNINGS

"How much longer will I have to count Mrs. Perriwinkle's pennies or listen to Mr. Jimmerson's dog stories?" Agonized Addie Carlson as she locked the door to the Whitford, Minnesota, bank.

It had been a long gloomy day, but she put on what she called her local smile. Mr. Reitan, the bank president, always reminded his employees to "look sharp and smile right," both in the bank and on the local scene.

A young, slim-figured blonde, Addie always walked the long five blocks to the post office. As she walked, she greeted former classmates. Some were veterans who had returned to Whitford three years ago at the end of the Korean War.

In the post office, she greeted two little girls from her church who were sporting new fall coats.

"They're so nice," commented Addie.

"We got them at Montgomery Wards," said the older one, while the younger child laughed and chanted "Monkey Wards! Monkey Wards!"

Addie smiled and left the post office to begin her trek to the egg station to meet her childhood friend, Marcia Olson, who worked there. Both girls lived approximately five miles from town and depended on Marcia's 1938 Chevrolet to get them to work and back home again.

A population of seven hundred, Whitford residents enjoyed their new clinic, a good school system, multiple stores, and a variety of restaurants. Both Ford and Chevrolet garages served to complete the picture of an attractive and successful town, while tall-grain silos on the edge of it defined Whitford's agricultural status.

But Addie felt she wanted something different. She wanted a chance to go to college and perhaps become a teacher who could help all students, but especially those whose problems were too difficult to solve alone.

As she reached one of the final blocks of her walk, she noticed Mr. Bakken overtaking her and matching her gait. He had operated the men's wear store for over thirty years and today, as usual, was dressed in a neat suit and hat.

"Addie," he said, clearing his throat. "I've been hearing something I don't like to hear about you."

"Such as?"

"That you will be leaving us soon to start college."

"Soon?" she asked, laughing at the hearsay always so prevalent in Whitford. "I guess I don't really know when I am going to start, but let me know when you hear."

Chuckling, Mr. Bakken turned onto another street, and Addie walked the final block to the station. Her feet were sore from walking and standing on high heels all day. She envied Marcia, who came out of the station dressed in dark blue slacks, a pink sweatshirt, and comfortable low-heeled shoes.

But she knew she would not like to have Marcia's job and wondered how her friend could check eggs all day. Marcia never complained, and Addie wished she could be more like her.

Marcia's brown curls bounced as she walked to the car to meet her. "I'm sorry I'm late," said Addie. "I had so much trouble balancing the books at Lorraine's window. It's my job until she comes back from her vacation and…"

"It's okay," replied Marcia as she started the car's engine. "It's not a problem."

The two were silent until they were out of the city limits where nature seemed to explode with autumn colors. The yellow-tinged corn, ready for harvest, waved with the rhythm of the wind, and the sunflowers' gold and brown heads followed the direction of the sun. Wheat and beans left only remnants of their days of glory, while neatly plowed black fields were reminiscent of Monet's artistic strokes.

The tolling of a bell interrupted their reveries. It rang in remembrance of Dr. Albright, a physician who had guarded the health of Whitford residents for over forty years.

"I just loved him," began Marcia, but her tribute was cut short as she swerved to miss a deer. It had darted out of the woods, missing the hood of the car by only one or two inches.

After adjusting to the excitement of the deer, Marcia brought her own exciting news. She and Les would be married soon. They would move into his aunt's house. Les's aunt's health was regressing, and she wanted to live with her daughter in Minot. Les was also planning on buying the forty acres for sale right across from Addie's home.

"We'd be neighbors if you and Steve built a house across the road," said Marcia. "I know he proposed to you when he came back from Korea. He'll do it again if you just encourage him."

Addie smiled at her friend. "There's no one I'd rather have as a neighbor than you," she replied. "But I really don't want to get married right now. I want to go to college and perhaps become a teacher."

She thought of children like Alice Jones, who had been in her own class at school. Alice was constantly teased because she was obese and had thick glasses. She had the highest scores in the school, but because there was no one to give her extra help in solving her other problems, she finally just gave up. She quit school and married a drifter who left her with two children and countless bills.

Recollections of childhood experiences often surfaced on daily rides—sometimes recalling school picnics at which Marcia played the parent role and supplied the food. Addie, always the teacher, brought the drinks. She served only water because that's the way they did it at school. Growing older, she realized that Coca Cola or Tab were too expensive for teachers to afford.

"Teachers aren't paid well," said Marcia. "Marriage would be a better option for both of us."

But Addie was adamant about the fact that she wanted both a teaching career and a husband. She knew of some women who were doing both if their school board allowed it. "They're proving they can have solid marriages and effective careers too," she said.

Addie wondered why Marcia's feelings about the subject were so different from hers.

They had very similar backgrounds but were poles apart on this issue.

As they drove without speaking, Addie thought of the rationale that had been spewed out to all girls in her high school. It was strongly suggested that girls should prepare for careers in teaching or nursing, but boys could enter any profession they chose. She remembered how Orrin Page flipped her pony tail and teased her by saying, "Get your typing skills in order, Addie, so you can work for me when I become rich and famous."

After brushing him aside, she had hurried to the chorus room where rehearsals would begin in ten minutes. They would be rehearsing the "Hallelujah Chorus," a difficult number by Handel, and she would be playing the piano accompaniment. She needed to practice but could think only of Orrin's words. Gazing at the music, she wondered about the women composers in Handel's time. There must have been some, she thought, and she wondered what happened to their music. Was it stuck inside them forever? And what about all the women who could have been great lawyers, doctors, or other professionals? What a terrible waste!

Marcia slowed the car to accommodate a cow from the Johnson farm that seemed to be considering a walk across the road. Danger averted, she said, "Addie, be realistic. You want the great American dream they talk about, but I feel I'll have it by living with Les, having his children and being a good wife and mother. This modern stuff is just not for me."

"But it will soon be the sixties, and women are now beginning to accept more challenges," countered Addie. "We need to work for more rights and—"

"Addie," interrupted Marcia, laughing. "You are turning into Susan B. Anthony right before my eyes. Let's change the subject. Who are you watching on TV?" asked Addie.

"I suppose my folks will want to watch *I Love Lucy*. There's a Marilyn Monroe movie on too."

"Great! That can teach us to be chased by men because we're so cute, not because we have a brain in our heads."

Sensing Marcia's impatience with her rhetoric, she changed the subject to crops and the poor yields. They discussed the unpredictability of the harvest and the pressure that went with it. "But the good Lord always seems to supply a balance that keeps farmers going," said.

Marcia. "Case in point, both your folks and mine have always farmed and—"

"No. My father was chief of police at Mountain View for six years. Then the city elected a new mayor who appointed a new chief of police. My folks decided to come back to Whitford and take over my mother's home farm because my grandfather had recently died."

As she turned into Addie's driveway, they heard the phone ringing. "That's Aunt Gert's ring," Addie said, "and I want to listen in to hear if they found their dog."

When Marcia stopped the car, Addie ran into the house but realized she was too late as she saw her mother hanging up the receiver. "The dog hasn't been found," said her mother, "but they still think he might find his way home."

Addie and Marcia's families were both happy with their telephone system that allowed them to listen in (rubbernecking) on both friends and relatives who were on their line. They knew each other's rings and often enjoyed listening to their conversations. Sometimes they even joined in the discussions. Whitford did not have a daily paper, so much of the social news was secured through rubbernecking. Because most Whitford families had only one car, they used the telephone more during the day and soon some people called it the Party Line.

As Addie hung up her coat and began to set the table, she commented on the delectable smell of the roast beef.

Her mother reminded her that when she was little she wouldn't eat beef for a long time because she thought her father had butchered her calf. Addie still wondered about it as they talked about the tough economic times.

"But we got by," said her father who had just come in from the field. "It was the year your brother died, and we thought life could never be good again—that is, until you came."

Addie smiled at her father, Thor Carlson, an immigrant from Norway who passionately loved his adopted country. He had scored high enough on civil service tests to guarantee him a good position away from the farm, but he loved country life and was happy living on a quarter of rich land with his wife, Marie, and daughter Addie. He also served on community improvement committees with other folks from Whitford.

As she approached high school graduation, Addie often thought of her future as a time of new beginnings that held promise and excitement. She was eager for it to begin.

Thor interrupted her musings to ask if she had seen Max and the other horses in the pasture on her way home. Thor knew she wanted to ride him and that her mother was cautioning her to ride before it became dark.

"I can hardly wait, Dad," she said. "When I'm riding Max, I always feel just like I'm riding into the sunset with Roy Rogers and Trigger."

After the meal, Thor left to locate Max's whereabouts. Addie and her mother washed and dried the dishes and stored the leftovers in the new Tupperware set. As they worked, Addie thought of the fable her mother had always used to instill the work ethic in her when she was only a toddler.

Derived from the Arabian version of "The Sky Is Falling," the fable was about a sparrow that lay in the middle of the road, feet up. When questioned by a horseman, the sparrow replied that he had heard the sky was falling, and he was holding it up. When asked if he thought he could hold up the whole sky, the sparrow stretched his little legs and replied, "One does what one can."

"I was just thinking about the sparrow," said Addie, as she put away the plates. "I'll always remember it."

"You should," her mother said, laughing. "You revised it so many times and used different characters—Chicken Little, soaring eagles, the Little Red Hen—I can't remember them all."

"I can, but I guess I like the eagle the best," said Addie, "because I realized the little sparrow tried so hard that he actually accomplished as much as an eagle."

"I never looked at it that way, but it makes me think of your music—especially piano. I know Mrs. Berg misses having you as her accompanist at school."

"I miss it too, Mom," she replied as she grabbed her jacket and ran out to meet her father and Max. Still reflecting on childhood experiences, she remembered Thor's words. With great pride, he would say, "When Addie grows up she will become a teacher."

The sky was darkening as Addie and her father trudged up the long hill from their neighbor's home. Addie's arm was around her father, and he was bent as though in pain.

Addie's mom ran to meet them. "What's wrong?" She asked, looking into his eyes for answers. Thor told her he went to Harley's barn to look for Max because Max went there a lot.

The door was wide open, and he saw Dr. Helland, who took Dr. Albright's place, in there. Thor's voice broke as he said, "He was cutting down the rope Harley had used to…hang himself."

"Why? Why on earth did he do it?" asked a stunned Marie.

Thor stopped walking and faced her. "His crop loan came due," he said. "He couldn't pay it, so the government took all of his grain and most of the animals to pay the loan." Thor's voice broke as he said, "He couldn't face it any more…so he just gave up the fight."

Addie, who had been teary-eyed during the walk, said that Dr. Helland broke down, trying to say he went to medical school to learn how to save lives, not to cut them down, and that he was sad but also angry, to think that good people could be driven to such actions.

Marie tightened her hold on Thor's arm and helped him onto the porch.

Quietly, she asked Addie to bring a shirt down to the sewing room and iron it because Thor needed something to wear at the Farmer's Union meeting the next day.

She knew the request was just an excuse to get her out of hearing range. She hated it, but she conformed with her mother's wishes. She wanted to hear all about everything that was happening, so she repeated her childhood act of hiding in a spot behind the cupboard where she could hear everything that was happening in the downstairs rooms and porch.

"Harley came to me this morning and wanted help," she heard her dad say. "But I couldn't do it." Suddenly a train whistle wiped away any sound. Hearing the porch door open, Addie ran to the sewing room and hurriedly ironed the shirt. Her parents retired to their room. She followed them upstairs to her own room and lay on her bed wondering about the future. Could her father be in trouble like Harley? She knew that both he and her mother had been looking for work in Whitford and outlying towns, but nothing was available.

What would happen if her father had a loan payment and couldn't pay it? Would the county step in and take away the farm, and maybe the house? Would the comfortable life they had been living be destroyed? If so, she wanted to stop it from happening. Her parents had always provided for her, but she was an adult now and felt a strong responsibility. But would she be able to give up her dream of being a teacher?

She pulled the covers over her head and tried to sleep, but couldn't. If her father were in trouble, she felt there was only one way she could help. It would mean taking the money she had been saving for over two years in order to go to school.

She got out of bed and went to her dresser drawer where she checked the amount of savings shown on her deposit slips.

The following morning was dark. Addie's disposition matched the weather as she thought of Harley and his family. She complained to her mother as she struggled to get into one of her outfits that she labeled Sunday Best.

"I'm tired of dressing up every day," Addie said.

"You dress for the job," commented her mother. "All the bank girls dress well and are greatly admired. In fact, I heard one gentleman ask who was that good-looking blonde who works at the bank. He was a nice looking man and, I think, Lutheran, too."

Addie usually laughed at her mother's suggestion that she marry Steve Janssen or someone like him who lived close to home, but today she objected. "That's not the life I want," she protested.

Addie realized her life in Whitford fell into an easy rhythm of work, a few dates, and Saturday mornings with Marcia. Sometimes the two would take the bus to Minneapolis to hear the McGuire Sisters or Bill Haley and his Comets or even Eddie Fisher and Frank Sinatra. Marcia's cousin, who attended the concerts with them, always invited the girls to stay with her until Sunday, when they took the bus back to Whitford. By all standards, it was a good life, but Addie yearned for college and a degree that could activate her dream of becoming a teacher.

As Addie entered the bank that morning, she was happy to see Lorraine back at her teller's window. Noticing that Mr. Allison's door was open, she knew he was ready to dictate, so she grabbed her notebook and entered his domain.

"We've got a lot of mail, and we've been delegated to send out the crop notices," he said, puffing on a cigar. "I thought insurance would do it, but I guess, they're swamped. Anyway, we'll have to speed things up."

Addie smiled. Mr. Allison's tasks were always urgent, but his dictation style was not swift. He smoked cigars with great expertise and blew giant smoke rings into the air. His thought processes were not quick, so Addie had time to watch the smoke curl and wind, like Hank's local barbershop pole. The stench of the cigars permeated her clothing, but all she could do was wait for a windy day and "air it and accept it."

The letters were easy and didn't take long. "Good work," said Mr. Allison as he lit up another cigar. "Now you can go through the files and write the names of people who are behind on their payments."

"Sure," agreed Addie with an outward smile but an inward groan. She hated writing letters with "payment due" marked on them and no available extensions. The government was demanding the impossible during times when crops were doomed to failure by the weather.

As she opened the file containing her father's records, she gasped at the balance due and quickly shut the file door again. Sitting motionless, she tried to calm herself. She would try it again. Maybe it was a mistake. Maybe she had looked at the Carlton files instead. After all, the two names were very similar. She opened the file again but shivered as she realized she would have to accept the fact that her father owed the bank $3,000, and due three years from that date.

Stifling a sob, she angrily shoved the file back into the vault and walked back to the office where she sat at her desk, motionless.

She looked at her watch. It was two thirty. She couldn't keep working on the files. It was too upsetting.

"What's the matter?" asked Mr. Allison, "Don't you feel well? Maybe you should take the rest of the afternoon off."

"Thanks. I'd like to go home early if I could. I think my ride can be here by three o'clock."

"We'll get at the delinquent accounts tomorrow."

Addie hurried to leave but was stopped by her former superintendent who had come to the bank to cash a check. "It's time for you to go on to school," he said, shaking his finger at her authoritatively.

"Next fall I'm hoping to go to the University of Minnesota," she answered, waiting for his approval, but instead, he shook his head forcefully, and said, "No. Don't wait."

That evening when Addie spoke of the superintendent's advice, her dad advised, "Do what you think best."

Her mother agreed, adding, "You'll be twenty years old in February, and you'll soon want to know where your future lies."

Addie pondered her problem. She knew her parents were in trouble and needed help, but she needed to hear it from them. Her dilemma increased daily. Her parents realized something was bothering her but felt that the pressure of getting ready for school was responsible. They evaded any discussion on finances until one night when Addie rubbered on a call from Aunt Julia to Mabel Anderson. Aunt Julia closed the conversation with, "Well, I hope Thor and Marie don't lose the farm over this debt."

Addie was dumbfounded that Aunt Julie could be so careless. She immediately ran to her father who was standing by the kitchen window, watching his cattle move out of the barn to pasture.

"Dad," she said, "I know about your loan, and so do a lot of people. Aunt Julia let it slip out while talking to Mrs. Anderson. I'm sure quite a few people were rubbering. They know that Aunt Gert always knows a lot of news."

As he turned from the window, she said, "I want to help."

"No," Thor said gently. "Going to college and becoming a fine teacher—that's your responsibility."

The debate continued as Addie tried to convince him that she probably had enough money to pay some of the loan. Maybe she would still have some left for school if she could supplement it with part-time work on campus. She knew that neither of her parents could find employment, but she felt she could pick up additional work in Minneapolis.

Addie's mother joined them with coffee and ginger cookies. "It's time to let Addie in on your plans," she said.

He agreed and told of his conversation with Bill Moen, a farmer who was also in loan trouble. Bill had seen an advertisement from a company in the state of Utah that needed help with construction during the wintertime. Bill was hired and was sure Thor could be employed by them also. Thor applied, was accepted and also elated to hear that the jobs would most likely be available in following years.

"I think this plan might work, but if it doesn't, we'll have to find another way. We'll work it out. Don't worry."

"We're a family," said Addie, squeezing his hand. "We're not a big one, but we are a family."

"And the sky won't fall," Marie said softly. "It might bend a little with the wind, but it won't fall."

In December, Addie boarded a bus to Minneapolis to enroll at the University of Minnesota, forty miles south of Whitford. She was determined to build a successful future and form lasting friendships.

As dusk approached, the Burma Shave signs and other advertisements sparked her interest. She was also impressed by the traffic that flowed so easily as people made their way home from work.

Addie had always been amazed with the size of the city, but she wasn't sure she would like to live there. She had enjoyed the short trips she and Marcia had made to hear celebrated artists like Frank Sinatra, but then she knew she would be back in Whitford the next day. As a student, she knew she could not be coming home many weekends because of the transportation expenses. Also, she needed the time to study. She wondered if she could survive living there long enough to get her degree. She hoped to find compatible friends and worried a little about her scholastic background. Would it be strong enough to help her pass the courses necessary to attain her goal of becoming a teacher?

As she gazed at groups of identical houses standing side by side with little space between, her mind raced back to the variety of farmsteads at Whitford. She felt a tinge of homesickness, but she pushed herself out of her worrywart doldrums just as she entered the University grounds. She was pleasantly surprised by the informal picture of students walking and talking together, enjoying each other's company. Some were going toward their dormitories while others moved toward classroom buildings. Most students were walking, but some rode bikes.

The bus deposited her at Pioneer Hall. She was met by Miss Lohn, the Dean of Women, an elderly lady with dark hair, brown eyes, and a welcoming smile.

"We're glad you're here," said the dean. "You'll have a room alone, but we won't charge extra." Addie sighed with relief. She knew she couldn't afford an increase.

"I've asked two girls who live next to you to show you your room and help you get acquainted," said the dean. "I see them coming now."

Ginny Nelson and Mary Lou Jones quickly claimed Addie as a friend. Ginny was a short, vivacious coed with curly brown hair and brown eyes. Mary Lou was a tall, willowy blonde, much quieter in nature than Ginny but with expressive blue eyes that seemed to light up in friendship when she saw you. Addie enjoyed being with them because they loved to do silly things like naming themselves the Three Graces—"Grace, Disgrace, and Dat Grace."

They painted their names on decorative wooden breadboards captioned "Friends Forever" and promised to always support each other. They sealed their vows with a three-way hug.

Addie felt lucky to have passed the Freshman English Competency Test. It enabled her to join Ginny and Mary Lou in English Literature. Ginny was a theatre major with a flair for applying theatrics to everyday living. She loved Shakespeare and would take some of his works home to direct scenes from them. She always cast herself in the assertive role with Mary Lou as the beautiful damsel and Addie in all other parts that held the play together. Ginny lived and loved theater and was determined to help her friends appreciate it as much.

As the three walked to class one day, Ginny clasped her hand to her heart and fell on the cold, hard pavement.

"What happened, Ginny? Are you all right?" called a troubled Mary Lou, who put her coat under Ginny's head.

"Do you think you can get up?" asked Addie, feeling Ginny's forehead and determining there wasn't a fever.

"One, two, three, up!" Addie called, remembering that her father always began his first aid with a pronouncement.

The following day, the same incident occurred. Mary Lou felt she should go to the doctor, but Addie felt Ginny was playing a game to feed her drama obsession. Addie planned to walk away from Ginny's dramatic scene.

It happened again, and Addie kept walking while Mary Lou stayed until Ginny opened her eyes and stood up.

"Why did you do it, Ginny?" asked Addie, who shook her head in amazement.

"We had an assignment in drama class to fall, and I thought I should have fun with it," she answered, laughing.

Addie enjoyed all of her classes, especially American History. Ginny, who also took the course, starred again as they studied Thomas Payne's "Give Me Liberty or Give Me Death" speech. In an unrequested surprise performance, Ginny stood and emoted the lines dramatically. The class laughed, but the instructor showed Ginny the door.

Geography Principles interested Addie in travel, and Library Science heightened her interest in books. She found the tumbling class annoying, but she loved auditioning for the chorus where she was soon welcomed as a new member. Her courses went well as the winter and spring quarters zoomed by.

School was over on May 10. Addie knew she would miss her friends, especially Ginny and Mary Lou but also knew she needed summer work to help finance her education.

"We'll miss you, Addie, but Mary Lou and I will both be here this summer, and we'll find an apartment where you can join us next fall," said Ginny.

"Great," said Addie. She was happy to move out of the dormitory. Expenses would be lower in an apartment, and she would enjoy living with Ginny and Mary Lou.

Saying goodbye, the three gave their traditional three-way hug, only now, it was longer and more intense. "You're the best friends I ever had," said Addie in muffled tones. Finally, they broke the embrace, and she hurried to catch the bus back to Whitford.

Soon she was back home, working at the grocery store and bank. Addie's father had paid over a third of the loan back and announced that he would have the same job next year. Addie and her mother were comforted by the news as their hopes for a bumper crop had dwindled.

On a beautiful day, shortly before she was to return to school, Addie told her mother she wanted to take lunch to her father. Marie, knowing how happy it would make Thor, fixed an extra special lunch of a ham sandwich, potato chips, and freshly baked chocolate cake.

Addie drove to the field where he was working and waited for him to drive up the hill to meet her. As she waited, she remembered the long drives she would take with him to adjoining fields, forming a bond that strengthened with years.

She waited a few more minutes, then decided to drive out to him. Panic set in when she saw that the tractor had hit a rock and overturned, pinning Thor's leg under it.

"I'll drive across the road to Olson's," she said. "It won't be long. I promise."

Shortly, John Olson and his hired man appeared, followed soon by the ambulance. As they freed his leg, John said, "We'll help harvest your crop, Thor. Don't worry about it."

Addie sat with her father at the hospital, comforting him by predicting he would have a swift recovery, but when Dr. Helland came to examine him, he said, "Thor, your left leg is broken and there are other injuries also. I don't like to tell you this, but there is no way you can go back to Utah."

Addie saw the pain in his face as he heard the doctor's words. Quickly she grabbed his hand and said, "Don't worry. We'll make it. Just as long as you get well, we'll be fine."

The worried look on his face frightened her. She had always felt he was indomitable, and now, she wasn't sure.

Chapter 2

EPIPHANY

Addie had enjoyed being home with family and friends, but summer working hours at both the store and bank were very tiring. She longed for her college classes and friends—also for whispered conversations between classes about new guys they had met or wanted to meet.

Back on campus, she worried about the loan. She felt she needed more work. Last year, when she entered the winter quarter, she could find only substitute kitchen help and a Saturday job at the nearby grocery store. Checking the employment vacancies, she found a stenographer position available on campus. She began working for Mr. Hollister, who dictated so rapidly she found it difficult to match his pace, even though she had always prided herself on her shorthand skills. Working both at the lawyer's office and grocery store seemed to dim her financial fears, and she enjoyed her courses and activities.

A trip to the college library one late autumn day raised Addie's level of campus excitement. Sitting at the table next to her was a boy she had admired from afar and wanted to meet. He was tall and handsome with reddish curly hair and freckles—a basketball star from Madison, Wisconsin, who had been recruited to play basketball for the University of Minnesota. He was concentrating so hard that Addie knew she couldn't get his attention. She decided to linger outside until he came out, hoping divine intervention would provide her an opportunity to speak with him.

After a few minutes, she felt that her actions were ridiculous, that he probably wouldn't want anything to do with her anyway. She started to leave, but just as he came out, she inadvertently dropped her notebook and the pages went sprawling over the sidewalk. The star retrieved them.

"Nice notes," he said, handing her the pages. "You must be in my English class."

"No, but I think you're in my biology class."

"No," he said with a boyish grin.

"I'd have noticed you." Addie blushed. "I guess it's someone who looks like you."

"Looks like me?" he asked, laughing. "There's no one on campus who looks like me." Pointing to his freckles, he said, "These are not the rage, you know."

"Oh, yes," said Addie, "I mean, I think they look nice."

"Really?" he asked. "Say, if you're going to the football game Saturday night, maybe we could meet afterwards and celebrate. It's the first game of the season. We're going to win, you know. By the way, my name is Eric Kleinert."

"I'm Addie Carlson. Of course we'll win, and sure, I'll see you after the game."

It was the beginning of a friendship that lasted throughout the school year. She made many new friends through Eric, whose outgoing personality, as well as his athletic ability, made him popular with everyone. Long conversations at the student union and parties after the game made the year a happy one.

One evening, as they relaxed in her apartment, she listened to him talk about wanting to own a bungalow with a picket fence and enjoy neighborhood picnics. He also talked about other activities married people enjoyed.

"Oh," said Addie as she looked at him questioningly. "You'd be married? And who would be that lucky gal?"

"I think you know," he said, as he took her in his arms. "And if you don't, you should." After a long goodnight kiss, he left.

As Addie closed the door, she knew she was smitten. She prayed he would let her know his true feelings about her soon. She felt he could be the soul mate she wanted. Maybe her search could end right here.

One Friday night, after supper at the Maid Rite Hamburger Shop, Eric suggested they go to see the movie *Blackboard Jungle*.

Addie was excited to see it. The show was about a teacher and had great reviews.

As they approached the Orpheum, they were surprised at the long lines waiting to get in. The only seats left were in the middle of the theatre next to a couple who appeared to be in their late seventies.

"I'm Ellie," greeted the lady as she welcomed them by motioning to the vacant seats. "I wanted to see this film because once upon a time I was a teacher."

"I'm. Addie…and I hope to be a teacher soon," she responded, shaking Ellie's hand.

Pointing at Eric, she said, "And this is my friend, Eric."

"Oh, you are such a nice couple," Ellie said as they sat down. "But I forgot to introduce you to Hubert," she added, pointing to him, seated next to her with his eyes closed. "He's my husband. Sleeps all the time, but I need him to drive." She laughed and said, "He's kind of a geek."

After a few minutes of film showing the antics of very disrespectful high school students, "Rock Around the Clock," a song from the film's sound track, began. The theatre exploded with action as viewers quickly left their seats and hurried to the aisles where they danced to the rhythm of the music.

"Come on," said Eric, taking Addie's hand and leading her quickly over the feet of the older couple. "Let's rock!" Addie found the intense gyrations and swift rhythms exhausting, but she was determined not to stop until Eric did.

After another film segment, the music played again, and even more people rushed to the aisles. Addie looked back and saw Ellie following her.

"What are you doing?" she asked.

"I want to rock, too," she answered as she forged ahead to the main aisle, moving her frail little body to the music. Addie smiled but quickly pushed her out of the way of a three-hundred-pound rocker.

"It's dangerous out here," cautioned Addie. "Maybe you better go back and see how Hubert is doing."

"Well, okay," she said as she shrugged her shoulders in disappointment, "but Hubert is asleep again. All he does is sleep."

"I'm not asleep," called Hubert above the din of people returning to their seats. "And I'm not a 'geek' either. I heard you called me a geek, and I don't even know what that is."

Ellie pushed her fingers through his silver hair. "Well, you're a cute 'geek,' Hubert, whatever it is," she said. Basking in her praise, he shut his eyes and fell back to sleep.

The movie was over, and Addie and Eric walked back to her apartment. She asked him in. "Ginny and Mary Lou are gone for the weekend. I have a surprise for you."

"I like surprises," he said as they entered the modest apartment. Eric sat on the worn but comfortable couch. Addie went to the kitchen and returned with a plate of chocolate chip cookies, she said were straight from Betty Crocker's fantastic cookbook. Eric smiled his appreciation and commented on both the looks and taste of the cookies. She asked if she should turn on Dinah Shore, but he settled back comfortably and said, "Let's just rest. All that rockin' wore me out."

"Our star player tired? Now don't go to sleep, or I'll have to tell the world that you're a 'geek.'" She kissed his forehead, then went to the kitchen to replenish the cookies.

At times, their evening discussions would be quite serious or at times light and fun-filled.

Tonight, the discussion was short. Addie gave the final statement.

"*Blackboard Jungle* was really scary for me," she said. "How students could bring dangerous weapons to class and use them to fight their teachers is incomprehensible. I could never teach in such a school, and I can't understand how anyone else could either."

Eric pushed a stray curl from Addie's face and whispered, "Stay here in the city where you and I can grow old together like Ellie and Hubert, only you'll be much prettier."

He kissed her and said softly, "I love you, Addie Carlson, more than anything in this world."

One afternoon in late April, Eric stopped at Addie's place to join her for a short walk before supper. As she opened the door, she smiled at his response to her new pink blouse and flowered circular skirt from the Montgomery Ward sales catalog.

"Hubba, Hubba," he said. "You look terrific."

As they walked down the street, she maneuvered a few twirls before Eric caught her and swooped her into his arms.

"Let me go," she said, laughing, but he carried her for almost a block, refusing to let her go until they met two small boys who stared at them in astonishment. As he released Addie, one of the boys asked her, "Do you have a sore leg?"

"No," said Addie, laughing.

"Then why was he carrying you?" asked the other.

"Because he's silly," answered Addie, bending down to meet their eye level. "Do you know what the word *silly* means?" she asked.

"Mama says we're both silly when we tickle her," he answered.

The other boy pointed to Eric, who was raising his arm and flexing his muscles with great authority. When the boys asked him who he was, he replied with a deep bravado, "I'm Jack Armstrong. I don't have a box of Wheaties with me, but tomorrow I'll bring some to your home for dinner."

"Let's go home and tell Mama," said one of the boys, tugging at the other. "I'll tell her."

"No! I will."

As they raced away, Addie, trying to keep from smiling, said, "You really shouldn't do that, Eric. Wait for me. I'll be right back."

Catching up with the boys a half block away as they turned into their yard, Addie called, "Wait, I have something to tell you."

Bending down again to meet their eye level, she said, "I wanted to tell you that my friend is not Jack Armstrong."

"He isn't?" asked one of the boys slowly, sounding as though he maybe on the verge of tears.

"Then he won't come tomorrow?" whined the other. "I really wanted him to come."

"I know," comforted Addie, "but I guess my friend was just pretending."

When asked if they had ever pretended to be Jack Armstrong, they nodded affirmatively. "See my muscles?" asked one of them as he raised his arms and flexed them just as Eric had shown them.

"Look at mine," said the other twin. "I eat my Wheaties."

Addie laughed and flexed her own muscles, saying that she could eat Wheaties too. "But you can't be Jack Armstrong," one said. "You're a girl."

Laughing and waving goodbye, the boys ran up the steps to their house.

Addie hurried to catch up to Eric. They were scheduled to meet Ginny and Mary Lou at the Maid Rite Shop for supper at five o'clock, and Eric was always punctual. Addie felt that both Ginny and Mary Lou enjoyed his company, and he seemed to reciprocate. He would often tease Mary Lou, calling her the most famous "femme fatale" on campus because his two roommates were smitten with her expressive brown eyes.

Mary Lou and Ginny questioned Eric about summer courses and then realized that all three of them were taking General Psychology from Dr. Swenson.

"Great!" exclaimed Addie. Turning to Eric, she teased, "That way I can check on you."

They all laughed, but after the girls left, Eric said, "I'm wondering how I can get to see you this summer, but with luck, maybe I can talk someone into lending me their car."

The end of the quarter came quickly. It would be difficult to say goodbye to Ginny and Mary Lou, but harder to face separation from Eric.

On the evening before she left, she walked with Eric along familiar university streets, talking about everything except the fact that she would be on the bus for Whitford in the morning. Coming to the jewelry store, they stopped to admire the rings.

"I should put this ring on your finger, Addie, and I will."

She looked up at him and asked, "Are you sure, Eric?"

"I'm positive."

The aged jeweler's voice cackled as he asked, "And when will you two be getting married?"

"As soon as I can afford the ring," answered Eric. "Soon, I hope."

He smiled and put his arm around her as they walked from the jewelry store to the door of her apartment. Feeling his closeness, she began to realize how difficult the summer would be without him. She wondered if it would be bearable.

"I'll miss you," she said softly. "We've got to find a way to see each other."

"We'll find it," he whispered as he reached down to give her a lingering goodbye kiss.

Watching him leave, she had a sinking feeling in her stomach, but she smiled when he turned and waved. As she walked slowly into her apartment, she pictured Eric as her husband, sitting at their kitchen table reading the newspaper.

Letters from Eric arrived biweekly in May, but they tapered off in June. Memories of his teasing, semi-flirtatious ways brought Addie a few moments of worry, but she always regarded his actions as harmless. Today she also brushed them aside, choosing to blame, instead, his heavy schedules and difficult subjects. She missed him greatly and wrote to him at least twice a week, always urging him to visit her at Whitford.

Finally, toward noon on a hot summer day on the first week of July, Eric walked into the store. Addie, who had just finished stacking a crate of canned peaches was very surprised.

"Eric!" she cried as she sprang up to give him a hug. "How did you get here?"

"I came with a fellow from my psychology course. He had to drive this way to pick up a term paper that his typist would have ready for him by noon. She only lives six miles from here, so he'll be back soon."

Addie introduced him to Mr. Hartel who had overheard their conversation. "Why don't you take a break?" he asked. "I think I can handle the traffic here."

She thanked him and hurriedly led Eric outside to the park across the street.

"It's so good to see you," Addie said as they found a bench that provided a small degree of privacy. "How are your classes? And how are Ginny and Mary Lou? Do you see them often?"

As her questions tumbled out, she wondered at his unresponsiveness. Usually he would laugh at her inquisitive nature, but today his serious mood puzzled her. Finally he said, "I meant to write you, but I couldn't find the words."

"You're usually pretty good with words," she quipped. "There were more in May than June, though. What happened?"

His silence, though only seconds, seemed unending. "Addie," he began, then stopped as he looked into her questioning eyes. "Addie," he began again, "I've always enjoyed being with you."

"And I've never been happier. What's wrong, Eric? Tell me."

"I'm seeing someone else," he blurted.

Speechless, she looked at him for confirmation that he had misspoken, that she had heard wrong. But as she looked at his serious expression and noticed his strong hands tightly clenching the bench, she knew what she had heard was true.

She took deep breaths until she was able to speak. "Who is it?" she asked.

"It's Mary Lou."

She searched his face, looking for clues to what had happened. "You and Mary Lou?" she asked in disbelief while trying to suppress the hurt as she pictured the two of them together—the man she loved and her trusted friend. She looked into his eyes until her own filled with tears that began sliding down her cheeks.

"Why are you doing this?" She sobbed. "You were going to buy me a ring, and I thought we were going to be married. You told me you loved me more than anything in the world. We talked about our careers and futures together. You even said you wanted us to grow old together."

"I'm so sorry."

"I just don't understand it. It's like my whole world has been swept away, and I don't know why, and I need to know. What went wrong, Eric? Tell me."

He didn't answer, but as she started to stand, he stood also. Facing him, she seemed to be looking at a different Eric through flashbacks of flirtations she had always considered harmless. The pouty "you don't understand" expression she had observed so many times, even at athletic contests, were now also transparent.

The epiphany caused introspection. Why had she failed to realize the scope of these problems before? Why had she been so blind?

More tears came as she realized the true character of the man she had chosen as her lifelong soul mate. She knew she would never again feel his strong arms around her or be able to run her fingers through his hair…and she would sorely miss the discussions about their hopes and dreams now gone.

They sat in silence—two still figures sitting on a park bench staring straight ahead at the people across the street of the small rural town. A woman in a blue hat chatted with the couple next to her. The tension of the situation she was experiencing made Addie want to flee her reality and join theirs, but she knew it was impossible. She had to find a way to deal with the numbness that engulfed her now and the heart ache and tears she knew would follow.

She heard a horn honk, announcing his friend's arrival.

"Goodbye, Addie," he said softly.

As he left she observed a butterfly with colorful wings flying from flower to flower.

Shutting her eyes, she sought comfort from the sun and from the quiet winds that brushed her cheeks. Momentarily they replaced the sting of reality.

Soon she walked back to the store. As she entered the building, customers milled around, looking for groceries. She strode past them and hurried to the privacy of the restroom where the tears finally came, relieving tension but leaving a slow, dull ache. She applied a generous amount of makeup to hide the puffiness of her eyes and the redness of her nose and cheeks. Forcing a smile, she opened the door and began waiting on customers.

When her dad came in for groceries, Mr. Heinen, who was emptying a crate of oranges, said, "There's not much business going on here today. Why don't you take the rest of the afternoon off?"

"Thanks," she said, putting on her sun glasses. "It will be good to get home early."

She told her father what had happened. He grunted in sympathy, mumbling an occasional, "That's too bad, Addie." She looked sideways at him, noticing how firmly he grasped the wheel and how his eyes never wavered from the road. This was also the way he lived his life, never straying from his course. He would set his goal and work for it. If he didn't succeed, he could accept the consequences and move on. *Why can't I do that?* wondered Addie. *I have many of the same genes, but I'm an emotional wreck.* The introspection brought more tears. She bit her lip, then, like her father, focused on the road ahead, as she watched the yellow line slip past as they drove.

When they reached their mail box, a short distance from the house, Thor stopped the car. He was starting to get out to check the mail when Addie said, "Wait, Dad. I wanted to tell you something. I want to come home to live and go back to work at the bank."

"Why?"

"Because I'm so unhappy at the university," she answered, looking down and trying not to let tears form.

"Why?" her father asked again. "Was it because a romance didn't work out as you wanted? That happens to a lot of people."

"I feel like such a loser."

He reached for her hand. "If you quit the university, you will be a loser. My advice is to go back to school and continue your plans to be a fine teacher, one who students will look back at and realize how much you contributed to their lives."

Addie noticed that Thor's limp was less pronounced as he got out of the car to retrieve the mail. He paused, then said with a smile, "When Addie grows up, she will become a teacher. Remember that?" he asked.

"Of course," said Addie, trying to smile.

When they drove the final few yards to the house, Lady, their dog, barked and jumped on them in an energetic welcome.

"We're home, Marie," said her father with his arm around Addie as if he were protecting her from the world. Her mother responded by announcing that she had just made fresh bread and Addie's favorite boysenberry jam.

Noticing Addie's glum demeanor and slumped shoulders, her mother stopped her chatter short.

"What's wrong?" she asked.

"Just the rest of my life," Addie answered softly. "Eric dumped me for Mary Lou."

Suddenly she burst into sobs. Her mother held out her arms to comfort her. Addie threw her purse on the table and rushed to them. "I'm so sorry this happened to you," her mother said, stroking Addie's long blonde hair. "But it will pass. I know how it feels."

"No, you don't." Sobbed Addie. "You don't know how it feels."

"Yes, I do," said her mother firmly. "I've been through it."

Addie stood back and looked at her. Her mother told of being engaged to a handsome young man from Madelia. "I loved him just as much as you think you love Eric." She smoothed the folds of her apron and continued. "He left for California to make money to buy a house on his land, but he fell in love with one of the girls he worked with. He wrote me a letter telling me the engagement was over."

She continued her story, describing how she thought she would die from loneliness and embarrassment, but she didn't because people were so kind. "They actually held up the sky for me," she said. She knew that the experience had made her cautious, but after a while, she met Thor and couldn't have asked for a better husband, a better life, and a more wonderful daughter.

Addie smiled weakly. "You were brave, Mom. I don't think I could be that brave."

"It wasn't bravery, Addie," she said as she handed her a handkerchief. "It was acceptance of something I couldn't change. It's a hard cross to bear, dear, but you'll become stronger because of it."

"Did you?"

Addie's tears mixed with laughter as she watched her mother answer the question by flexing the muscles of her long, bony arms.

The last thing she remembered before going to sleep was her mother standing in the doorway saying, "Sometimes crosses can become crowns."

After work, a few days later, Addie was pleased to find a letter in her room from Ginny, who wrote,

> I've thought of you so much and worried about you. How are you coping? I wish I could be with you, but I desperately need to get my work handed in by the end of the first session so I can get to my boyfriend's graduation in Peoria on the 10th. I'm sure I wrote that I reconnected with him at our school homecoming a month ago, and he wants me to come back to Peoria and get married. He'll be in law school, and I'll find a job.
>
> Another surprise—Eric and Mary Lou are moving to Madison, Wisconsin, where Eric will study engineering. He always wanted to go there, but when the University of Minnesota offered him a basketball scholarship, he decided to take it. Now his doctor is advising him to quit playing because the injuries he has suffered from football have weakened his system, and it can't take any more abuse.
>
> Addie, I can't bear to lose you as my wonderful friend and confidante. I'll send you my address as soon as I know it. Please write often and come to Peoria to visit.
>
> With love,
> Ginny

> P.S. Even though Eric is approaching marriage, he still seems to feel it necessary to impress all of us with his questionable magnetism, so I can't help thinking you might be fortunate to have had the "bump in the road" now, even though it is hard to accept.

Addie checked the mail again, looking for a note of apology from Mary Lou. Didn't her friend care at all about how she was feeling—about the rejection she was experiencing? She put Ginny's letter in her purse but couldn't stop crying. She called to her mother, "I'm going to bed now."

"So soon, Addie? It's only eight o'clock."

"I know, but I'm tired and tomorrow is Friday. The weekends have been crazy lately."

Each step she climbed to her upstairs bedroom seemed weighted with her dilemma. She quickly changed into pajamas and pulled back the quilt her mother had made her for graduation. Climbing into bed, she pined, "It's too hard, God. How do you expect me to handle all this?"

The words "accept and gain strength" seemed to penetrate her consciousness as though God and her mother had joined forces. She knew the advice was good, but the tears would not stop as she sobbed. "I just don't think I can be that strong." Propping another pillow behind her, she buried her head in its softness as she tried to shut out the problems of her world.

Responding to customers' needs in the store kept Addie focused on her work, leaving little time to dwell on her own concerns. At times, however, she would find herself thinking of Eric's wide smile and his tousled hair. She wondered when his attraction to Mary Lou had begun. Could it have been when he was still dating her? She bit her lip as she visualized the two of them together. To block out her thoughts, she sometimes became overly talkative to customers, while at other times her mind wandered as she gathered up their groceries, often forgetting what they had ordered. Mr. Heinan acted like he didn't notice, but she knew he was aware of her breakup with Eric.

He would try to lift her spirits by telling her jokes she didn't think were funny, but she would laugh and carry on the game.

On a warm, summer day in mid-August, Madge Hansel, a high school classmate, stopped at the store.

"Can we go for lunch?" she asked.

"Sure," answered Addie, as she finished stacking the bread shelves. "I can leave in ten minutes."

"Cozy Café okay?"

"Sure. See you there."

Addie had always liked Madge, an attractive brunette with an outgoing personality, but she had never associated much with her. Madge belonged to the town group that socialized after school while Addie rode the bus and formed most of her friendships with rural classmates.

Entering the café, she saw Madge waving her arms from a back booth.

"It was a nice surprise to see you at the store this morning," said Addie as she slid into the booth. "Can you believe it's already over three years since we graduated? I haven't touched base with anyone from our class this summer. The ones around here are married and busy."

"I know. They all have babies or toddlers to care for," said Madge, handing Addie one of the menus. "I don't have any kids, and I'm glad I don't. As of today, I don't have a husband either." Averting Addie's gaze momentarily, she continued softly, "Maybe you heard I filed for divorce. The final papers came today, and I really need to get out and see people tonight. I don't want to go with a couple, and I was wondering if you would go with me."

Surprised at the news and feeling the urgency of her request, Addie answered, "Why, sure. Where do you want go to?"

Madge described Harold's Place as a nice club with a large dance area and many tables to accommodate customers. She also mentioned that a few of their classmates would be coming back for the weekend. "We can have a mini reunion."

"I'd love to go," said Addie.

Time went quickly as they shared a hamburger meal special. Madge didn't refer to the divorce again, but turned the conversation to high school memories and mutual friends.

They agreed that graduation seemed to be a long time ago, and they discussed the different places their friends were living. Some lived out West, some in New York, and many in Minneapolis. Madge pushed a glob of mashed potatoes to the side of her plate.

"Why didn't you go on to school?" asked Addie, looking at her intently. "You were our valedictorian."

Madge replied, "I fell in love and got married. It was a mistake. My husband had other interests—cute ones. I hope it never happens to you."

"It already has," replied Addie as she described her break with Eric. "It flattened my world like a deflated balloon."

"I had the same feeling," said Madge. "But it's getting better for me, and it will for you too."

Smiling, she quipped. "Balloons can reinflate you know. In fact," she said, as she grabbed a lone celery stick from the vegetable plate, "I think mine will inflate big time next week." She spoke of an uncle who was financing a trip to Africa for her, a kind of "cheer up" gesture, she supposed, but she was excited to be going and seeing all the different animals.

"The people, too," said Addie. "I'd love to go to Africa someday."

Addie reached for her purse and stood. "It was good to talk. I wish I could stay, but I have to get back to the store. I'm really looking forward to tonight."

As she hurried out the door of the café, she thought about Africa and remembered a dream she had when she was only thirteen. She had heard God's words, so strong yet gentle, saying, "Go to Africa." And she wondered why.

As the group entered Harold's Place, the nickelodeon was blasting "Mack the Knife" while loud voices sought to communicate over the din of the machine. The pavilion afforded room for many couples to dance. Tables were situated around the dance floor.

"I reserved a table," said Madge, leading the way.

Addie was delighted to see customers she knew from both the bank and the store, as well as classmates she hadn't seen since graduation. But as the evening wore on, her energy drained. She was exhausted. Last night, she had watched her clock's hands move slowly through the night.

A tall man with dark brown hair approached the table. She recognized Russ Sielstad, who operated a large dairy farm and was marrying Tracy Johnson. Tracy had worked with Addie on the school paper.

Madge said, "Russ is doing very well in the dairy business."

Addie asked, jokingly, "Really? Does he shoot spit balls at his cows?"

"You remember, don't you?"

"How could I forget?" exclaimed Addie. "They flew through the air, and I was the main target. I hated to go to English class because I knew Russ would be there with his rubber band. Miss Polsom was our teacher. Remember how when she turned to write on the blackboard, Russ sent the paper whirling?"

"Hey! I think I heard my name," called Russ.

"We were reminiscing," said Madge, motioning for Russ to join them. "Hey, Addie Carlson! I had quite a case on you in junior high."

She looked at Russ, who was at least six feet tall with brown hair and a ruddy complexion that gave him a strong outdoors look.

"I thought your case was against me," she said, laughing.

Russ apologized for the spit balls and said he just wanted to get her attention. "I wanted you to notice me. That's the way we did it in junior high. But now we're grownup," he said. "Let's dance."

Thankful for the dance course she had taken last quarter, she tried to follow his energetic two-step, but after two dances, she said, "Russ, I think I'm too tired to do another dance. I really should get home. It's getting late."

He looked at his watch and said, "Tracy and I are also going soon. We'll be happy to give you a ride home. Tracy has early church tomorrow." Laughing, he added, "I never stay late because my cows are early risers."

After explaining her early departure to Madge, Addie said goodnight to the people at her table and stepped outside to wait for Russ and Tracy. Russ drove to the front of the club in a sleek black Mercury.

"Sit in front, Addie," said Tracy. "There's plenty of room."

After reminiscing with Tracy about the Whitford school paper, Addie commented, "I hear that you two are getting married soon. That's great news. Congratulations."

"I'm a lucky man," said Russ, smiling at Tracy.

Looking at their happy faces, she thought of Steve Janssen. Had she made a big mistake by not accepting his proposal? Why did she feel she had to scout the world before settling down? She probably should have stayed right here and married Steve.

Tracy's voice broke through her musings as Russ stopped the car in front of her house. "How about you, Addie. Is there anyone significant in your life?"

"Significant," repeated Addie. "That's a wonderful term. But to answer your question, the answer is no, not now, but there was until a month ago. Then he found someone more significant."

"I'm sorry," said Tracy, patting her hand.

"Please…no pity."

"No pity," Russ agreed. "Just friendship. Actually, I think you should be happy, Addie, that this 'change of significance' came before you married the guy. Madge is the one I feel for. She didn't have that luck."

A heavy silence followed, finally broken by Russ as he opened the car door for Addie and said, "There are lots of guys for you to choose from. As many as there are stars in the sky."

"The sky is pretty dark tonight, Russ."

"I know, but it will clear. Remember that."

Addie laughed to herself. So much about the past weeks seemed dark and murky. The evening sky held only a few stars, and they were so dim it was hard to remember that nights like this could be followed by a brighter tomorrow.

"Thanks for tonight and for the ride home," said Addie. "I really enjoyed the evening." It had been a nice evening, she thought as she walked up the cement steps to her house.

The support of her former classmates gave her comfort, and she felt a strengthening of the bonds they had shared in early childhood. The "bumps in the road" were becoming smoother. She hadn't thought of Eric all night and realized he wasn't dominating her thoughts as he had before.

The lights were still on as she entered the house. Her dad had gone to bed, but her mother was listening to the news.

When she commented on the nice time she had enjoyed with her friends, her mother said happily, "I'm glad you got to see them before college starts."

Her mother's words jolted Addie into realizing that school would begin in only two weeks. She needed to begin planning.

Chapter 3

EDUCATION 401

"Do you like going to school, Johnny?" asked Addie as she made a sandwich for herself in the kitchen of Ellen, her new landlady.

"Nope," said Ellen's seven-year-old son. He shook his head vehemently. "I don't like school."

"He likes to go to religious school on Wednesday afternoons," said Ellen, "but last week, he sneaked off with a friend and went to the Catholic school instead of his own."

Johnny, holding both hands to the heavens, said, "Mama, when I grow up I think I want to be the Pope."

Addie smiled. She enjoyed living in the home of Ellen and Johnny where she had moved after Ginny and Mary Lou left. She rented two rooms in the attic and had kitchen privileges. As living alone was more expensive, she needed to carry three jobs. She continued working at the grocery store and typing for Mr. Hollister at the law office. On her third job, obtained through the campus health services, she would spend evenings, when called, with the county nurse, Jan Olson. She sterilized needles and helped with correspondence.

Jan, a roly-poly fun-loving woman, laughed and joked a lot. She impressed Addie with her ongoing humor, but also with her love for her profession.

"When did you decide to become a nurse?" asked Addie one night when they were both sterilizing needles.

"When I was a little girl, I guess. I've always wanted to do something helpful and I thought it would be exciting to be a nurse. Of course, I also thought I would marry a very rich doctor."

"And you didn't?" asked Addie feigning shock.

"No, Louie is a plumber, but I wouldn't trade him," she answered, smiling. "And I love my career, Addie. The human body is such a wonderful instrument—the way it all works together. If I can help someone overcome their problems and help get things working right again, I feel as thankful and happy as they do. It's such a glorious feeling."

"I think I'll have the same passion for my career," said Addie, softly.

Job number three at the grocery store, however, was a different matter. Saturdays were long and hard because there were so many customers on weekends, and as usual, people ordered at the counter and the clerks trotted after the groceries. At night, Addie's legs ached so much that if she didn't have a date or other plans, she would treat herself to a hamburger at the Maid Rite and go home to soak her feet.

Even with carrying three jobs, Addie wondered if her money would hold out. She tried not to worry but, rather, to focus on her present jobs. She might possibly have to add another job during her senior year if the crop yield didn't improve. She might need to help her father pay back the money he owed.

At times, she looked at the sky and thought it must be bending downward, that it wasn't really holding up. She felt the fatigue of the jobs and the stress of her studies. She wondered if she could make it to graduation or if she should quit now and try again later.

After class one day, she went to her apartment to rest a few minutes before going to work at the store, but the phone's constant ringing heightened her irritation. She didn't want to talk to anyone. She needed rest and not conversation, but the phone's loud shrill sound caused her to angrily answer, "Hello."

It was her mother who was speaking so fast, at times almost breathlessly. She told her Mrs. Berg was retiring and moving to

Arizona because of health problems. Since there were very few piano teachers in Whitford, she wondered if Addie might consider teaching her students during the summer. She said she had just raised her rates to $1.50 per lesson and recommended that those prices stay the same.

"I told her you would be in summer school because you wanted to pick up the credits you needed since you didn't start with the fall quarter. But I also said I thought you might be interested in teaching on weekends both in the summer and during the next school year. What do you think?"

Addie's exuberance could not be contained as she realized her life was back on track. "I think it's a wonderful idea, Mom," she shouted. "I'm quite sure I can be back at Whitford early on Friday afternoons to begin the weekends of teaching piano. I know Mrs. Berg gave lessons at school and students were allowed to leave class for a half hour...so please give Mrs. Berg my thanks and tell her I'll be home next weekend to make arrangements. This will help so much."

Looking up at the sky, Addie whispered thankfully, "It's not going to fall."

Addie's senior year involved student teaching at a laboratory school affiliated with the university. Intent on making a good impression on Miss Lewis, the supervisor, she donned her "Sunday best" dress, seamless stockings, and three-inch heels. She was ready, she thought. She smiled as she approached Miss Lewis's desk, but Miss Lewis was not smiling. She asked Addie what she was doing today, what she had planned. Addie, feeling uncomfortable, answered that she had planned to observe her. Miss Lewis asked, "Why didn't you contact me?"

"I guess I didn't know I was supposed to," answered Addie, now visibly shaken.

"Miss Carlson," the supervisor said with authority, "if you had a job as a teacher, wouldn't you make some contact with the school and wouldn't you make some preparations before you appeared on the scene?"

"Why, yes, of course," answered Addie.

"So then wouldn't it be logical to assume the same thing here?"

Not waiting for an answer, Miss Lewis said to the class, "Miss Carlson will be helping me teach your English class until the end of the school year. She is not prepared today, but perhaps tomorrow she will be."

Addie, hurt and angry, sat down. She must have missed some direction that said, "See your supervising teacher before your arrival date." She was visibly upset, but she forced her attention on Miss Lewis who deftly introduced the class to creative writing.

The following day, she was definitely prepared. Miss Lewis seemed happy with Addie's presentation on the art of essay writing. Addie had researched the "Voice of Democracy" contest and was assigning a paper to be due in one week. As she looked at the class, a heterogeneous group of fifteen children of junior high school age, she became eager to know their backgrounds, their interests, and their dreams for the future. Some were professor's children, some were there because they lived in the neighborhood, and two of them were from the Children's Home downtown.

The due date of the essays arrived. Jeff Stubenoff, a shy looking boy, did not turn in a paper. Addie asked him to stay after class, thinking he didn't have time to write or probably didn't like the project.

Jeff, shifting his feet uneasily, said, "The reason I didn't write it is because I don't believe in democracy, and what's more neither does my dad! If we're all born so equal and this democracy is so great, why does my house have dirt floors and my friends have linoleum? Some even have carpets."

Addie admired the small, forlorn figure standing before her, courageously stating his convictions.

"I understand what you are saying," said Addie. "There are some things that need change, especially when they concern wages and jobs, but we can try to work for those things through people who represent us." She paused a moment, then continued, "Jeff, I'd like to work for change that would make you feel different. Would you be willing to work with me?"

He looked inquiringly at Addie. Suddenly a smile appeared as he said, "Sure." As he left, she called, "Why don't you write down some of the things that you would like to work for. Try to think of those that would help you and your family, and write a paragraph on it. Okay?"

Jeff nodded affirmatively.

Addie beamed. She thought she saw a faint smile from Miss Lewis's lips, and she hoped this could be the beginning of her redemption.

Her students became very important to Addie, especially the disadvantaged and those with other difficulties. Carrie, a fifteen-year-old from a Children's Home had been taken from her own home while her mother was recovering from a nervous breakdown. Carrie already walked the streets of prostitution. She had never known her father, but she loved her mother and lived for the time when they could reunite. Anna, also from the Children's Home, had a borderline IQ. She was shy and needed social contacts. Jim, a professor's son who lived near campus, talked constantly to anyone who would listen. Although only eleven, Jim could possibly enter high school the following year to escape the boredom he was experiencing at the junior high school level. Addie, however, worried about his social readiness, and Miss Lewis agreed that careful consideration must be given to that aspect of his development.

Suddenly, the school year was almost over. Addie was not looking forward to another summer in the grocery store at Whitford, but Mr. Heinan was losing his main clerk of thirty-five years, so she had agreed to fill in for the summer.

In May, Addie invited all the girls in her class to a Mother-Daughter Banquet at a local church, but only Carrie and Anna could attend. May was a busy time for many students who were involved in sports and music activities.

"You two look so lovely," said Addie as she met them at the church. Carrie wore a blue figured dress with a lace border on the neck and sleeves, while Anna wore a pink tailored suit. Addie couldn't help wondering what life would offer these two. Their hurdles might be great ones, she thought—especially Carrie's.

The girls seemed to enjoy the lunch of cashew chicken hot dish. Anna was delighted to see a plate of snickerdoodle cookies. "Mama used to bake them every Saturday," she said. They also welcomed the attention they received from the ladies of the church. The event seemed to end too soon for all of them. Carrie was radiantly happy as she whispered to Addie, "I'm going home, Miss Carlson. Mom is out, and we'll be together again. Isn't that the greatest?"

Addie squeezed her hand and smiled back at her. She wished she could match Carrie's happiness and be sure that everything would be all right.

"Say," said Addie as she was about to leave the girls, "how about a picnic before Carrie goes?"

"Great," said Anna. Carrie agreed enthusiastically.

With papers to grade and reports due, Addie overlooked the picnic plans until one morning, when she awoke to a beautiful day and said, "This is a day for a picnic." She thought of her promise to Anna and Carrie and dialed Anna's number. The call was answered by a supervisor who said that Anna's family was visiting for the day. Then she quickly dialed Carrie, but was informed she had left yesterday to live with her mother in St. Paul. Dejected, Addie could not stop reprimanding herself for waiting until this late date, but there was nothing she could do to remedy the situation. She tried to forget about it. She was done with classes, and it was a week until graduation. So she packed her suitcase and went home to work at the store.

As she relaxed on the couch after a busy day of work, a television news report grasped her attention.

"A fifteen-year-old girl was found dead in an alley in St. Paul. She had been engaging in prostitution."

Addie screamed, "No!" as Carrie's name flashed across the screen.

Carrie's funeral was held in a mortuary in St. Paul. Addie felt a strong urgency to make the trip to say goodbye to this beautiful child whose chance for a real life had been cut short by tragedy. She was surprised when her mother tried to dissuade her from going and having more contact with Carrie's friends and family. Addie put her arm around her mother and said, "Mom, do you think that after the way you and Dad have raised me that I could change because of a short association with other people who didn't have my luck? Carrie was a student I was trying to help, but time went by too quickly." Her voice broke as she said, "There wasn't enough time, and now, she's gone forever, and all I can do now is to go and say goodbye."

"Don't worry, Mom," she said again as she left to join her father who was waiting to drive her to the bus depot.

Carrie's mother came to meet her. She was too upset to talk much, but she thanked Addie for coming. "Carrie always wanted to be a teacher…just like you."

Addie gazed at Carrie, who wore the same lovely blue dress she had worn to the Mother-Daughter Banquet. In her hands was a yellow rose. As she looked at her, Addie's anger began to build. Why had the system failed this child? Why had she been allowed to return to her mother when both the mother and the environment were unstable? So many questions flooded her mind, questions with no definite answers. She had not slept well since Carrie's death. She kept reliving the Mother-Daughter Banquet time when they had laughed and enjoyed the day. She chided herself again for not following through in time to schedule the picnic she had promised.

The principal from Carrie's school in St. Paul approached Addie. "I was really afraid of what would happen if she came back," he said, "but I had no recourse to stop it. I was shocked but not surprised to hear of Carrie's death."

Speakers at the service were the principal and the minister of the church that Carrie would sometimes attend. Their remarks were general, as though they had never really known her. At the conclusion of their remarks, Addie asked if she could say a few words.

"Of course," said the minister.

She reached the podium, adjusted the microphone and began to speak.

"I met Carrie for the first time when she came to my classroom to volunteer to help clean my erasers. I had just told my 'sparrow story' to her class, a story that encourages helping others. Needless to say, I was impressed as well as appreciative of her help. I had many good conversations with Carrie during 'eraser time.' She told me how much she loved her mother and how she wanted her to get well so she could return home." Addie paused. Emotions surfaced as she thought of the result of Carrie's return, but when controlled, she began again. "I just have to tell you this about Carrie. When I watched her study in the classroom, she would always wind her finger around her hair. This seemed strange to me, so I asked, 'Carrie, why do you keep winding your finger around your hair when you study?' She laughed when she answered me, 'I really can't tell you. Maybe I'm trying to wake up my thinking cap?'

"The last time I saw Carrie was at the Mother-Daughter Banquet that we attended together. It was such a beautiful day, and Carrie looked so lovely. We laughed a lot and had a wonderful time. She was radiant because she was going home to be with her mom." Addie struggled noticeably to get through her final thoughts. She spoke slowly. "I think we are all just specks on this universe, and I truly believe that the wind has blown Carrie straight into her Savior's arms. Carrie," she concluded, as she turned toward the coffin, "we love you and we miss you."

Saying goodbye to Carrie's mother, an aunt and uncle, the principal and the minister, Addie left the smallest and saddest funeral she would ever attend. As she boarded the bus, unsettling thoughts crowded her mind. *How could this have happened? Why are beautiful children like Carrie given "no chance" tickets to life? How can this be changed? What can I do? What should I have done? There must be something I could have done. What kind of a teacher am I? I'm a failure.*

Tears covered her cheeks as she sought comfort in the sparrow's words, "One does what one can."

But tonight there was no comfort.

College commencement exercises were on May 12. She enjoyed the walk with the other graduates from Northrop Field to Memorial Stadium where the graduation ceremony would be held.

"Well, this is a big moment for us," shouted one inductee.

"It would be bigger if we had jobs," quipped another.

Addie wondered how many of them had jobs and how many felt as she did, that the world seemed a little more threatening now because the future was not sure.

As the president of the university spoke, Addie gazed at Harold Carey in the row ahead of her. He was a fine student, but a rather dull, pedantic soul who had asked her to the prom by saying, "All you have to do is sit there and look lovely." She accepted, and the evening turned out to be as dull as she had feared.

Many of the graduates were struggling to sit up straight and listen. Mona Haggendorf, Addie noticed, was still with her act of leaning forward and giving the impression she was absorbing every word. Perhaps, Addie mused, she forgot that this speech didn't count toward her grades.

Sitting on the end seat of the third long row of graduates, Addie was able to see a few of her former instructors seated to her left. They weren't brimming with enthusiasm either. There was Beth Simmons, the art instructor who loved purple. Sure enough, a little purple scarf peeked through the collar of her gown. Next to her was Mr. Johnson, one of her music education instructors who had talked her into getting a minor in music. "English and music degrees are a good combination," he had told her.

Mr. Hassel, her biology teacher, was conversing quietly with the colleague next to him. She remembered the acrid smell of formaldehyde that was always present when her class studied the anatomy of the crayfish and the frog. Despite Mr. Hassel's excellent teaching skills, she had found the subject to be difficult and was happy to pass the course.

Her musings were interrupted by everyone standing, so she stood up as fast as she could. Reaching up to secure her own cap, she inadvertently knocked Harold's cap to the ground. He scrambled to pick it up as fellow students laughed and, seemingly, enjoyed his dilemma, thus proving to Addie that college does not necessarily promote maturity.

With her diploma in hand and the tassel on her cap turned to graduate status, Addie joined in the recessional march. The commencement was finally over.

After hugs to classmates, Addie joined her parents.

"Mom, you're sporting a new hat. I can't believe it," commented Addie, knowing her mother's frugal ways.

"Your father insisted. He wanted us both to look acceptable at your graduation."

"You would be acceptable any way you dressed." She thought of the hardships they had faced, from crop failures to the death of an infant son.

"Aunt Julie is in Toledo with her daughter," said her mother. "And Aunt Helen would have come, but the twins got sick." The twins were eight and were difficult for Aunt Helen, now a widow, to raise alone. She had married at thirty-four, brought the twins into the world the next year, and lost her husband to cancer soon after.

"I understand," said Addie, "and that's all right. As long as you two are here, I won't complain."

Time went quickly as they enjoyed a steak dinner at the Radisson Hotel in Minneapolis, serenaded by the Golden Strings. There was much to celebrate. Addie and her father had paid off the bank loan, and she was debt-free from college. Addie watched them leave in their 1950 Plymouth hoping that crop yields would improve, and they could soon afford to buy a new one.

Alone, Addie pondered her own future with a little anxiety as she did not know where she was going or what she was going to do. That feeling, however, soon changed to excitement.

There's a vast, beautiful world out there, she mused, *and I'm ready to climb some mountains.*

Her first mountain locale was Roseland, a town of ten thousand people. It was located forty miles south of the university. She had contacted a teacher's placement agency that sent her papers to Roseland. A week later, after a short personal interview, she received a letter from their superintendent stating they would be happy to welcome her to their faculty. She would teach tenth-grade English and senior high school speech.

Chapter 4

ROSELAND

In August of 1960, Addie secured a loan and drove to Roseland in a light blue Chevrolet she had purchased with the guidance of her father. She felt uneasy driving alone on this maiden voyage but realized she had to start shouldering responsibility for every facet of her life, including transportation. The fact that bus connections between Roseland and her home were terrible sparked the purchase, and her father assured her that the car, though not new, was a wonderful one.

The radio is great, she thought, *but I hope the engine works too.*

Having a flat tire on the way did little to change that feeling. She skidded over to the side of the road and sat assessing her problem. Soon a car stopped and out stepped a pleasant-looking man dressed in jeans, a plaid shirt and a cowboy hat.

"Hello, miss," he said brightly. "It looks like you've got yourself a little problem?"

"A flat tire," said Addie, glumly. "I just bought my car and am already having problems."

"Oh no, just a little inconvenience, that's all. Do you have a jack?"

"Yes," said Addie, taking it from her trunk. "It's awfully nice of you to stop and help me."

"No problem," he said. "It's just a little 'courtesy of the road' that I like to practice when I see a need. Yesiree, we all need a little help sometimes and if I can extend a little assistance I'm happy, mighty happy, to do it."

He gave her a beaming smile and returned to his car.

Addie drove away thinking of the kindness the man had shown her. Suddenly she bolted in the car seat as she realized that the jack had not been returned. Wittingly or unwittingly, it was now many miles away in the opposite direction.

I'll have to do better next time, she said to herself.

As Addie continued her trip, she saw acres of sprawling farmland. Nearing Roseland, she admired the beautiful golf course. Upon entering the city she was further impressed by the attractive facades of the business places and the neat sidewalks and streets.

Three blocks down from the business section was the school. Looming above other buildings, its rich red brick looked beautiful as the sun's rays danced on the exterior.

She drove to Mrs. Hendrickson's home close to the school, where she would be renting a room for thirty-five dollars a month. *So reasonable*, thought Addie, *when I think of my annual salary of thirty-five hundred.*

"It's nice to meet you, Addie," said Mrs. Hendrickson, a middle-aged lady with a cheerful smile but, Addie thought, inquiring eyes. "I hope you'll like it here."

"I will," said Addie, smiling. "I'm so excited about teaching, and I'm glad to have a few days to get ready. In fact, I think I'll walk over there this afternoon."

"It's not very far, just a couple of blocks," Mrs. Hendrickson said, pointing to the school from her window.

At the door of the school, Addie met Mr. Hensrud, the principal, who escorted her to her room.

"It's nice and big," he said, "and has lots of room for bulletin boards."

Addie smiled weakly. Bulletin boards were not her favorite, neither were big classes. She remembered that her laboratory classes at college ranged between fifteen to twenty students.

When Mr. Hensrud left, she tried her desk chair. Feels good, she thought. She opened some of the large windows to get rid of stale air that permeated the building that had been closed most of the summer. Then, she began making plans for the first day of school.

As the students filed into the classroom and took their seats quietly, Addie was favorably impressed.

"Welcome to tenth-grade English," she said, smiling. "You'll be joining me every school day for the next nine months, so we should begin by becoming acquainted. My name is Miss Carlson. The spelling is on the board, so you shouldn't have any trouble if you need to write it, especially if you're Norwegian."

Noticing a few smiles, she continued, "I'll call roll and see if I can pronounce your names. Please correct me if I'm saying yours wrong because names are important, but before roll call, I should tell you that there are three fables on your desk. I think you might know that a fable teaches a lesson, so we'll see what one of them has to teach today. After roll call, you can read all three, but pay special attention to 'The Sky Is Falling' because that's the one we will be discussing."

Toward the end of the period, she felt that most students had read the fables, so she announced that time was up.

"Who would like to begin telling the story?" she asked.

"I would," called a girl from the back row. In a loud, clear voice she began, "Well, this little sparrow is lying down and a soldier comes along and sees him and asks what he is doing. The sparrow says, 'Well, I heard the sky is falling and I sure don't want it to fall, so I'm holding it up.'"

"Nice summary," said Addie. "Could someone finish it?"

A small, bespectacled boy in the front row raised his hand. "That horseman ridiculed the sparrow by asking, 'Do you think your spindly legs could hold up the sky?' But the sparrow just tightened his little legs and said, 'One does what one can.'"

"Very good," said Addie. Looking at the class, which was still attentive, she added, "I've always liked this fable. I even try to apply it to my life. I don't always succeed, but I do make an effort. As I was planning for today, I wondered if we could possibly bring the wisdom of the sparrow to our classroom, so I would like to ask you this question, as a class, how do you think we could hold up the sky for each other?"

No one answered.

Addie paused, then asked again, "How can we hold up the sky for each other?" Slowly, the answers began coming.

"Working together."

"Helping each other."

"Working toward a goal."

"Yes," said Addie, "and who does the work?"

"Everyone," chimed the class.

"You're right, it includes everyone," responded Addie. "There are no exceptions. The sparrow did not say, 'I can't build a new building or design a sky ceiling or anything else,' or 'I don't know how,' or 'I'm not strong enough.' He said, 'One does what one can.' And that's what I hope we can realize this year, that if we all do the best we can by working together and helping each other, we can build success for everyone…and maybe, at times, we can even raise our levels of performance from that of sparrows to eagles."

The class is starting out so well, thought Addie as the bell that governs the lives of both teachers and students rang sharply and class was dismissed.

One of the first students who claimed Addie's attention was the class clown, Jimmy Lake, a sandy haired boy with thick glasses and a high energy level. Addie looked at him as a diamond in the rough, especially after hearing his speeches. His speech on dating was impressive as he entertained the class with points such as "We all know that dating is expensive, so what you do is take a short girl to the movies and get her in for half price—or if that doesn't work, take a big enough girl so that you get in for half price. After the movie, you have to have a treat, so you do the 'cozy act.' You share a malt, and when she isn't looking, you pinch her straw."

Addie searched for a humorous cutting from "Midsummer Night's Dream" and finally settled on "Pyramus and Thisbe." His comedic performance earned him a superior rating at the state contest. Now he was a class celebrity as well as a clown whose humor one day even set Addie into laughter as he dramatized being an eagle by flapping his arms on the way to the door. The rest of the class, seeing Addie's reaction, began flapping their arms also as the bell rang, and they all flew down the hall to their next class.

On the day of Halloween, the speech class, led by Jimmy, had planned a costume party with a prize for the most creative one. Many were unusual, but Jimmy, as a ghost with jingle bells, brought down the house.

When the contest was over, the students left the classroom to remove their costumes, but Jimmy had one act left. On the way to the "change room," he stopped at Mrs. Jolard's classroom, threw open the door, shook his bells and shouted, "Boo!" The class roared but Mrs. Jolard was ashen white. She was sixty-five years old and had just gone to see her heart doctor. She had only four words for Jimmy—"Go to the office."

Mr. Hensrud, the principal, called Addie to the office to pick up her erring charge. He told Jimmy to apologize to Miss Carlson, and as he left, Addie saw laugh crinkles forming around his eyes.

"I didn't know Mrs. Jolard was sick," Jimmy said, fidgeting nervously, "or I wouldn't have done it."

Addie comforted him by saying that Mrs. Jolard was not ill but had just gone for a checkup and was frightened by Jimmy's noisy entrance.

Addie thought Jimmy had learned a lesson from it, when asked, he replied, "Yeah" with a big sigh of relief, then added, "You have to know your territory before you perform."

"That's right, but you didn't follow the rules so it's detention after school. See you then."

By detention time, Jimmy was back to his lighthearted self as he took out his English book and began working on the next day's assignment.

One of the students entering Roseland High that fall was Carl Potocki, a 6'8" junior from the neighboring town of Slayt. He looked uneasy as he tried to fit his tall frame into one of Addie's desks.

"I'm sorry about the desk, Carl. We'll have a different one for you by tomorrow. Think you can hold out?" asked Addie.

"Guess so," he said, shifting his feet back and forth, trying to find some measure of comfort for his long gangly legs.

When the bell rang, Addie went to the teacher's lounge to make a phone call and was surprised to find Coach Hendrix, the basketball coach, so excited.

"We have the tall man I've been praying for," he said, raising his arms in a cheering gesture.

"He must be good," said Addie.

"He will be," answered the coach in a tone that Addie knew meant business. "He played well for Slayt last year, and he'll be better this year, maybe he'll even grow another inch or two."

"Why is he going here instead of Slayt?"

"They changed the boundaries, which is a break for us. By the way, I looked at his transcript, and I really don't know how he got to play last year. He needs help with academics, especially English, in order to qualify for any sports. Could you help us?"

"Sure, I'll have him come in before school."

Carl was agreeable to early morning sessions, but the progress was so slow during the first week that Addie wondered if he could ever qualify for the team. It would take him so long to read the short section she had assigned that he would often slam the book shut with the words, "I can't. I just can't do it."

"It's the reading, isn't it?" asked Addie. Carl nodded.

"Are the letters scrambled?"

"Well—yes."

"Are some backwards?"

"Yes," he said, nodding his head and looking uncomfortable.

Sensing his frustration, Addie chose her words carefully. "You are not alone with this reading problem, Carl, and I think that, like many others, you might have a visual learning problem that causes you to learn in a different way. We'll just have to adopt a different learning style." She smiled at him, adding, "I'll help you with it, OK?"

With tones barely audible, he muttered, "I'm just dumb."

He started to leave but was stopped by Addie, who asked, "Have you ever heard of Albert Einstein?"

"Sure," he answered as he turned around to face her.

"He was learning disabled. Then add Winston Churchill, Thomas Edison, Hans Christian Anderson, and many other famous people. You're in excellent company. Some of the brightest people in our history. No, Carl, you're not dumb," she said firmly. "Like them, you're very intelligent."

Addie knew she couldn't handle his problem alone. She had to be sure her diagnosis was correct, so she called in the school psychologist.

"You were right," he said after testing Carl. "I'll meet with him today and explain the problem. The exercises he should be trying are starred in a book I'll leave with you."

Addie thanked him, wondering how she could plow through those books when she needed her time that week for constructing midsemester English tests and finding declamation materials that would entice speech students to begin work on their selections.

Midnight oil again, she thought wearily.

Carl labored with the new approach to his studies, and as he became more proficient, he became more confident. By the first of December, his grades had improved enough for him to make a late start in basketball. He worked hard on the sport and Addie thought Coach Hendrix seemed pleased with his progress.

During Carl's senior year, midseason tickets for Roseland basketball games were at a premium. People crowded the gym to watch Coach Hendrix's exceptional team led by a 6'8" athlete who could pass, shoot, and slam dunk, seemingly at will.

In late March, Carl received a basketball scholarship offer from the University of Minnesota.

"The doors are opening for you," said Addie. "Coach Hendrix tells me that the university wants you to sign a letter of intent to accept their offer.

Shuffling his feet, Carl said, "I've never thought much of going to college, Miss Carlson."

"But why not? You're becoming a good student, and you're a wonderful athlete. Why wouldn't you seize this opportunity?"

"I like my horses and the farm, and I've always thought I'd go back there after graduation. We have two hundred acres. That's a lot for my dad to take care of."

Addie wanted to discourage the farming, but she held back. This was Carl's decision.

Why should she inject her feelings?

After school, Carl's dad brought him a snack because Carl had forgotten his lunch on the bus. He had eaten only a bite or two of Eddie Dale's sandwich, which was not enough to carry him through a rigorous practice.

Addie was walking to the principal's office when Carl stopped her and introduced her to his dad. After Carl left for practice, Mr. Potocki thanked Addie for all the help she had given his son.

"Carl is studying hard and doing very well," said Addie, smiling, "and our school is benefiting from his athletic ability."

"He is doing better than I ever thought he could in both studies and basketball," responded his father. "But he's troubled. He doesn't know what to do about this letter of intent that Coach Hendrix wants him to sign with the university. Carl isn't sure. What would you suggest?"

"With Carl's ability, I definitely think he should sign so that he doesn't pass up a great opportunity."

"Later, if he decides against it, I think the intent can be erased. It's not cut in stone."

Mr. Potocki seemed relieved, and the following week Carl sent the university his letter of acceptance.

After a successful senior year, both in basketball and academics, Carl left for the university. He regularly reported his activities to Coach Hendrix who told Addie he was lifting weights and exercising to gain strength. The basketball season began in November, and all of Roseland was waiting to see Carl make his debut on television. They were disappointed. He spent most of his time on the bench, but when he did get on the floor, he couldn't seem to make his shots or get the rebounds. Even his passing was hesitant.

"What's going on, Coach?" asked Addie.

"I don't know, but it must be a lack of confidence thing. I'm sure the coach has been on him pretty hard. Write him a letter of encouragement, will you, Addie? I've written him, but you English teachers are better with words, and you've been through a lot with him. Maybe you can help him out of this slump."

Before she had a chance to write, Addie received a letter from Carl full of complaints:

"My playing stinks and my coach is constantly on me. I can't seem to do anything right. I've lost my heart for the game, and I'm thinking of going back to the farm."

Addie answered by return mail:

'So you're playing stinks right now. Do you think it will be that way forever? Don't you think that many people have disappointing experiences that make them want to quit? That's not you, Carl. Remember that you are playing in a different league now, and you can't run away with all the honors as you did in high school because the line between your abilities and your teammates or opponents is a very fine one. Your coach is 'on you' because he wants to help you cross that line."

Addie watched every game on TV and though he didn't play a lot, she thought she saw a slight improvement as the season advanced.

At least, she thought, he's hanging in there.

One day, Addie found another letter from Carl in her box, thanking her for her help and enclosing two tickets for the university pre-Christmas game.

Addie was excited about going. Coach Hendrix and his wife, who also had received tickets, couldn't go because they were celebrating their twenty-fifth wedding anniversary on that day. They gave their tickets to Addie, who invited Carl's parents and Eddie Dale, Carl's best friend.

Addie drove. The game was at two o'clock, but they were there before lunch and were met by Carl, who greeted them warmly. They had time for just a short visit before Carl had to leave for a team "shoot-around" in preparation for the game.

As he left, he called to Eddie. "When I get home, we'll scrimmage, okay?"

"Sure. I might even have to beat you."

Addie laughed at the two friends' simultaneous shouts of "You're on!"

As it was soon time for the game, they left and took their seats in the upper middle section of the arena, a location that afforded good visibility. The band was playing the "Minnesota Rouser" while smiling cheerleaders in short skirts led the supporters in cheers for the university team. The audience sang the "Star Spangled Banner" and the game began.

The first half opened at a slow tempo. Both teams had trouble scoring, and the university was being outrebounded. To make matters even worse, their two top scorers were already in foul trouble.

The game droned on, but suddenly, the opposing team caught fire and went on a run, scoring ten points so quickly that the crowd was on their feet in disbelief. The score was thirty to fifteen as the first half ended.

Addie spent the half time intermission worrying about Carl's folks and how disappointed they would be if their son didn't soon get the nod to play.

Midway through the second half of the game, the split widened to a score of forty-five to twenty-six. Then it happened. With eight minutes left of the game, Carl got the nod and ran out on the floor. Addie thought he looked like he had been pent up long enough. He seemed poised for action.

Acting as the point guard, Carl brought the ball down the floor. He was all over the floor, at times dribbling backwards. The tempo of the game increased. He slam dunked baskets, he shot from the side, he successfully maneuvered to open spaces where his shots would go in easily. His teammates seemed to catch his fire and the split narrowed. With only one minute left, the opposing team had the ball. They were one point ahead, trying hard to stall, but suddenly, the crowd stood and cheered as they watched a university player steal the ball and throw a long pass to Carl who quickly made the final basket.

The fans were jubilant. Carl's parents jumped to their feet. Addie couldn't have been happier as Carl passed over that fine line to success.

Addie was surprised and happy to see Nina Olson on the faculty at Roseland. They had been friends at the university and were active in the campus Lutheran Association. After graduation, Nina had begun teaching at Roseland where she married Bill Olson, an associate pastor of a nearby Lutheran church.

Nina entered Addie's room one morning before school and saw her looking out her window almost transfixed. As Addie motioned her to come closer to the window, she said, "I can see a lot from this window, but there are things I don't like to see. For example, there's Emily Harris by herself, looking so forlorn while six groups of girls make sure they are far enough away so they won't have to converse with her."

Stepping away from the window, she continued, "Nina, she reminds me so much of Alice Jones, and Alice is one of the reasons I wanted to go into teaching. Everyone teased her because she was so bright and wore thick glasses... After watching her suffer, I wanted to become a teacher because I thought I could help students who are bullied and neglected. Now, here I am with another Alice Jones, only with a different name, and I don't know how to hold up the sky for her."

As she walked to her desk to take out the test papers for her first hour class, she said, "I really like all of my students, but if I can't seem to help them feel the importance of accepting each other and treating each other with respect, then I'm a failure even if they improve scholastically. Some days I really want to quit teaching and other days I think I've made some gains. It's like a rollercoaster."

"Sounds like a typical teacher one," responded Nina, smiling.

"My personal life is on the same roller coaster," continued Addie. "I need to find a soul mate to share my life with, and I want to find him soon. I'll be in my late twenties shortly, and I've always heard that by that time you're on your way to spinsterhood. I feel that marriage and teaching are the two things I really need in my life. The teaching role is satisfactory. In fact, sometimes I feel a little like Emily, alone and unhappy."

"Addie," said Nina as she walked toward the desk. "I have a window just like yours. Every morning, I go to that window and look up at the unending expanse of the universe. Then I realize that if I have a creator that powerful, I certainly think he'll help me solve my problems…and I know he'll help you decide what to do about Emily. Keep the faith, Addie," she said as she left to return to her classroom.

"Wait, Nina," Addie called. "I need to ask you something."

Nina returned, saluted, and said, laughing, "At your service."

"Nina, do you think Bill was actually called to the ministry?"

"I think he was. From the time he was seven years old, he knew he would be a minister."

"I've never told this to anyone else before, Nina, but when I was twelve years old, in the middle of the night, a voice so loud and clear and powerful said, 'Go to Africa'! It jolted me right out of bed. I didn't know what to do, but I remembered reading about Samuel in Sunday School. He thought the Lord had called him in the middle of the night, but Eli told him to go back to bed and see if he called again. Well, he did call again for Samuel but not for me, so I put it in the back of my mind; but every now and then I think of it and wonder… Nina, do you think it was a call? Or maybe a dream?"

"No one can tell you the answer," responded Nina. "Maybe you'll have to go there someday and find the answer for yourself."

"It's not in my plans right now," said Addie, "but if I get a chance, I would like to go."

Later in the day, Addie was still thinking of Emily. She needed to get closer to her and to other students to assess their needs and determine what she could do to help them.

Again she went to the window and decided to open it and take a few breaths of fresh air. Using her imagination, she visualized a morning group of girls mingling and playing without Emily, who was still alone. She shut the window with a bang and returned to her desk. She sat in silence with no productive thoughts occurring until she visualized the group again, but now, one thing was different. She, herself, was there too, mingling and talking with her students. Why hadn't she thought of this before? Instead of meeting her students at the main door at eight thirty, she thought she would meet them outside at eight o'clock on mornings when it was feasible.

On the first day of her personally revised schedule, she was greeted with surprise.

"Miss Carlson, what are you doing here?" they asked, crowding around her. "It's not time to go in yet."

She smiled and answered by singing a few bars of "Getting to Know You."

"That's what I'm doing here," she said. "I thought I'd come a few minutes early and get to know you. I can't seem to do that in English classes of thirty-five students. But let's just start with an old game 'Rover, Red Rover.' We'll need two captains. How about Mary and… Emily. Choose your teams quickly, girls, and have fun. Today I have to leave early, but I'll be doing some watching from the window."

Mingling with her students became a ritual she enjoyed. She began to know more about them—their families, friendships, feelings, likes, dislikes, and hobbies. Most students expressed themselves freely except for a few—one of whom was Emily.

One day, Addie stopped Emily and asked, "What is your favorite pastime, Emily? I didn't get to talk to you about it very much outside."

Emily surprised her by smiling and answering, "I just love dancing."

Addie dragged one of the school's ancient phonographs into her room. She asked the girls to come up front. "Boys, you can work on tomorrow's assignment in class because the girls and I will be rehearsing a dance from Greece to go with one of our units. Girls, I'll show you the steps, then you can repeat them."

Some were managing the steps, though awkwardly, others were joking and laughing at each other's attempts.

"Keep trying," encouraged Addie. "It will come." *But where is Emily?* wondered Addie.

"Do it again," she called to the group. Then she saw Emily. She was dancing in and out of the cloak hall with beauty and grace far past her age.

"Who taught you to dance?" asked Addie, who joined her among the coats.

"No one. My dad isn't home much, so I dance a lot in front of the TV. Sometimes I copy steps I see and sometimes I make up my own."

"Do you ever work out routines, Emily?"

"I try."

"Any jazz?"

"Yes," she said, laughing.

Turning to the girls, she asked, "And how many would like to form a dance team with Emily as captain?"

A few hands came up but not enough for a team until Addie said, "Maybe we'll dance at some basketball games during intermission."

Most of the others' hands shot up quickly and practices soon began.

But she needs help with clothing too, thought Addie. She resolved to talk to Emily's father whom she had met at the grocery store where he sometimes worked. One night she saw him leave the store with two friends and quickly go toward a bar next to the store.

"Mr. Nelson," she called, following him. "Could I talk with you?" The middle-aged gentleman stopped and turned to face her.

"It's about Emily," she said. "You've probably noticed she needs more clothes for school, and I can get some from the county as well as other places. Do I have your permission?"

"Do what you want," he said. "Do what's best for her. She ain't got no mother, and I ain't got no wife. Emily is all I've got."

"If I may ask, what happened to your wife?"

"She left us when Emily was a baby," he said as he lit a cigarette.

"I'm so sorry," said Addie.

"But Emily likes to dance," he said, "and she's good at it."

"I know," said Addie. "She's the leader of our dance team."

"Great," he responded.

When she started to leave, he called, "Wait. Who are you?"

"I'm Addie Carlson, Emily's teacher. I met you at the grocery store with Emily."

"Oh, I didn't remember," he said as he tipped his hat, then joined his friends.

Another cool March morning, Addie thought as she put down her pencil and rushed to the physical education door to escort her group down the hall and back to class. As the students filed into her room, Addie asked, "Where is Richard?"

"We forgot him," they said, laughing.

Walking to the window from where she could see the athletic field, she reported, "He's coming now, but he isn't laughing, but I suppose you wouldn't either if you had snow to contend with and were in a wheelchair, and your legs didn't work."

"We'll go get him," offered a few contrite class members.

"No, he's almost here, but maybe you can apologize in some way, especially the monitor," she said looking at Frank Stark who fidgeted uncomfortably.

Addie opened the door and Richard entered. She followed him to his desk to give out material for class and noticed that on his desk he had two baseball books—a sport she knew he loved.

"Looks like you like baseball, Richard."

"Oh, yeah." She knew that he, along with the other boys in her class, had a passion for the sport.

That night, Addie phoned Rex Steele, manager of the local Jets Baseball Club, whom she had met through Nina and Bill.

"Rex, I need a favor," she said.

"Already?" he asked, jokingly, "We just met. No—seriously, what can I do for you?"

"How about a personal appearance at one of my classes? I have a roomful of baseball fans and one boy in particular. He has cerebral palsy, is in a wheelchair, but loves baseball and is very knowledgeable and—"

"I'm in," interrupted Rex. "And if you let me come on Monday at any time that suits you, I'll bring along a fellow who knows everything about baseball, and he can quiz your class."

"That's great," said Addie, holding up her non-telephone hand in a silent but jubilant cheer. "Can you be there at nine thirty? That's my first class."

"We'll be there," he agreed.

Promptly at nine thirty on Monday, Rex Steele and his friend, the manager of the local Jets team, marched in as Addie played "Take Me Out to the Ball Game" on a piano temporarily moved into her room.

Jet schedules were distributed and discussed, then Jim Lawson was introduced.

"I'm happy to be here," Lawson said, "but I don't want to put your education at a standstill, so I'm going to give you a test."

The class laughed.

"Here goes," said Lawson. "I want to know how many games the Twins won in 1962."

"Eighty-five?" asked one student.

"No. Someone else guess."

"Seventy-six?"

"No. Someone else?"

Waving his hand frantically, Richard called, "Ninety-one."

"Correct," called Lawson. "Here's another question, what shortstop led the American League in assists in 1962?"

After many faulty answers, the nod again went to Richard who answered, "Zoilo Versalles."

"Good job, young man," ruled Lawson as he took a ball from his pocket and knelt by Richard's wheelchair. He placed the ball, signed by some of the Twins, in Richard's hands.

"You're a number one champ, Richard Blake," he said.

Turning to the class, Lawson said, "I have one more question for you. Besides the 'Whitford Jets,' who is your favorite team?"

"Minnesota Twins!" everyone yelled. Addie quickly began playing the Twins' song as the guests exited.

The class gathered around Richard and asked, almost in unison, "How did you get to know so much about the Twins?"

"I read a lot about them, and I like to watch baseball," he said.

"We have a club that meets on Tuesday night after school when we can trade baseball cards. Why don't you come?" asked one of the boys.

"I might do that," answered Richard, smiling. "I've got lots of cards."

As they left, Addie looked at her roster of remaining class sections and wondered how these students could be inspired to accept differences in classmates and work effectively with each other. She struggled constantly with this concept of inclusiveness that seemed to improve only through exhibitions of talent shown by students like Jimmy, Carl, and Emily.

But what about the others?

On some days of unsuccessful efforts to improve the situation, Addie knew the nights would probably be long. Then she would toss and turn, wondering why it took so much effort to help students become more acceptant of each other. She often remembered her father's words, "We are a nation of immigrants, Addie. We need to respect each other and work together to keep our country strong." Then, after reciting a poem she learned in third grade, she would finally drop off to sleep.

Don't Give Up
by Phoebe Carey
If you've tried and have not won,
Never stop for crying.
All that's good and great is done
just by patient trying.

After lunch on a beautiful November day, students stood in the school lobby, talking about the coming holidays. When the bell rang, they hurried to their classes. A few minutes later the secretary from the principal's office delivered Addie a note. After reading it, she shut her literature book quietly and told her class to line up by the door. "We're going to the auditorium." Anticipating some type of a holiday program, students talked and laughed until the principal stepped to the podium looking grim and authoritative. The noise stopped. He cleared his throat and began to speak, but he stopped to clear his throat again. The students thought he must be under some type of pressure, but they were not ready for his words describing the assassination of their president, John F. Kennedy. Gasps of disbelief and shouts of "No! No!" rang through the audience as teachers tried to comfort the students and guide them back to their classrooms.

"It's hard to realize we have lost our president," Addie said as she took a notebook out of her drawer. "People react differently to grief. Some want to talk, some prefer silence, some like to write. In addition to how they feel, many will tell where they were when they heard the news, who they were with, and other remembrances.

"You may want to write something today. You don't have to, but sometimes it helps to put your thoughts on paper."

Many took out their notebooks and wrote—some through tears. Others put their heads down, and a few stared vacantly into space. Many contributions were posted on the school walls as creative talents emerged through the grief of a stricken nation.

> As a nation we'll strive to embrace your precepts
> and follow your lead.
> We'll protect our country and serve with love
> and help from above.
> John L.
> Grade 10
> November 22, 1963

Friendships were easy to make in Roseland. Often the young unattached business people socialized with single teachers to make life more enjoyable and interesting. Some weekends they would congregate at Ben O'Reilly's place to lick their collective wounds and play cards or watch TV. Ben, whose parents were deceased, lived in the family home.

The O'Reilly's, a prominent Catholic family who had lived at Roseland since the 1920s, were considered part of the town's history. Ben's father had been a doctor, and his mother had directed the church choir for many years.

They raised three sons, all of whom had attended St. John's University near St. Cloud. Jack, the eldest, was killed in the Korean War. Michael married and settled in Connecticut, where he worked in medical research. Ben, the youngest, majored in business, came back to Roseland, and worked in the county auditor's office. When the auditor retired, Ben ran for the office and won easily.

On Saturday nights, the group would often go for dinner at a local club and mingle with the community. Addie enjoyed the entire group, but she was most attracted to Ben O'Reilly, a tall, slim, bespectacled man with brown hair and hazel eyes. As county auditor he had a reputation for being both brilliant and honest, and his name was often mentioned as a prospective candidate for mayor of Roseland. He loved literature and philosophy, a welcome change for Addie who was tired of listening to an ophthalmologist friend who seemed to see things only one way, and Jim Meyers, a science teacher who never forgot that he once played ten minutes on the university basketball team. Jim was an avid sportsman who talked about sports a lot in his classes. One day, to his chagrin, his name was listed in the news paper's "offense" column because he was caught fishing without a license. The group at Ben's, tired of his braggadocio personality, silently cheered.

Verona Lawson, an elementary school teacher, also joined the group quite often. Most of the elementary teachers were married, so Verona relied on the social group "a la Ben" for companionship. She was a pretty brunette with hazel eyes and a voice with a babyish twang, but she was always friendly and, seemingly, happy. She hung on to every word that Jim Meyers spoke whenever he entered the room. That anyone would have such a crush on Jim was incomprehensible to Addie, but the couple seemed inseparable, and they soon announced their engagement.

Sharon Middleton, the vocal music teacher, had a golden voice and golden hair that framed a pretty oval face and flirtatious blue eyes. She loved to go to the local club and frequently went on weeknights with a wealthy farmer, but on weekends, she usually left for home to continue her relationship with a boyfriend she had been dating for three years. To the "a la Ben" group, it seemed as though Sharon were vaulting between her two romantic interests with no plans for a solid landing.

Larry Jones, the assistant coach in both basketball and football, was by all standards, Addie thought, a very nice young man. He had a dry sense of humor and could sometimes come up with memorable "one liners" that would highlight the evening. He was of medium build, always had a crew cut, and was friendly to everyone, but with a little extra attention for Verona.

"I wish Verona would get together with Larry instead of going with Jim," said Addie to Ben.

"Quit matchmaking," he responded. "Verona is of age and capable."

"And vulnerable," added Addie. "It's too late anyway. She and Jim are getting married in the spring, and you and I will be attendants."

"They haven't asked me," said Ben, shaking his head.

"They will."

"Does that mean a tux?" he asked with a worried look.

"Yes."

He groaned.

Joining these regulars sometimes was Betsy Smith, an attractive young brunette who was recently divorced and in need of friendship. Addie's selfish nature emerged when Betsy appeared. Betsy engaged Ben in long conversations, and Ben didn't seem to mind his role as her private counselor.

Lyle Hood worked with Ben in the county auditor's office. He was a tall, good-looking man with red hair and glasses, extremely polite but seeming to carry his formal public relations personality into everyday conversations, which made some of the group think he was a bore.

Without the encumbrance of dating, Ben and Addie found it easy to discuss their futures honestly and platonically. They conversed easily and openly on most subjects, including religion. Neither would marry for the sake of marrying, neither would marry outside of his religion, and both felt not finding a suitable mate to be a distinct possibility.

"We all have crosses to bear, Addie," Ben said one evening after most of the group had left. "Maybe that will be ours."

"Perhaps," she answered, thinking of her mother's statement that crosses can sometimes become crowns, "but it can't be as heavy as the cross of an unhappy marriage."

She looked at the clock. "It's getting late, Ben," she said. "I'll have to go. I sing in the choir tomorrow at early church."

Ben walked her to her car. When he cleared his throat and said, "Addie." She thought he might ask her for a date, but he didn't. He paused, then started again. "Addie, are you going to the football game on Monday night?"

"I might, even though I don't understand the game completely."

Ben suggested getting a group together, as they often did, and he would explain the plays she didn't understand.

"Great," responded Addie. "It will be fun."

The Monday night of the game was balmy and beautiful. Townspeople, students and teachers flocked to the field to support Roseland in its effort to keep an undefeated record. Ben, Addie, Verona, Jim, Betsy, and Lyle came as a group to enjoy the evening.

A few high school students approached the group and greeted them. Then they gave their full attention to Ben, asking when the Boy Scout badges would come. Ben thought they would be there by Wednesday and told them to be sure to be at the ceremony at eight o'clock Friday night to accept their honors.

As they left, Addie mentioned that she didn't know he worked with Scouts but wasn't surprised because she knew he had been an Eagle Scout.

"Hey, Ben!" called a voice from up higher in the bleachers. Ben looked around to see Mike O'Gorman approaching. Mike was a fellow student at St. John's but now lived in Milwaukee.

"Mike, it's good to see you," said Ben, enthusiastically shaking his hand, "I haven't seen you since St. John's."

"I don't get back here very often. I live in Milwaukee. I'm married and have two kids. How about you? Did you become a priest?"

"No, I thought about it and started the course work, but I changed my mind. Guess I wanted to live a more normal life. I like my job here. I'm the county auditor and I enjoy the work."

As he left, Addie laughed and said, "I should go to more games with you, Ben. I could find out a lot of things about you."

Suddenly a roar went up from the crowd. Roseland scored another touchdown and was on its way to victory. Ben was explaining the plays in the second half of the game to Addie when Jake Bakken made a spectacular touchdown. Addie jumped up, yelling, "Bravo! Jake, Bravo!"

"This isn't Carnegie Hall," said Ben, smiling.

"Everyone should be on his feet yelling for Jake," retorted Addie. "He's the hardest working kid in school, and he's working that hard just so he can come out here and play. He deserves a bravo, even from Carnegie Hall."

"Okay," said Ben. "Let's all stand up and cheer for Jake."

The small group of six stood up and yelled for Jake Bakken. The more elite sports-goers looked back and smiled.

The game ended with a 60–20 victory and the group left the field listening to the chatter of Jim Meyers, who kept reliving his high school football days in full glory.

Spring came quickly. Basketball was over and baseball and track held the limelight.

Students succumbed to spring fever and waited patiently for the 4 p.m. departure bell.

Addie scheduled her final tests for the middle of May and conducted a thorough review but was extremely disappointed in the test results.

Calling Verona's number, she agonized, "Verona, I need to do something tonight. There's a good movie, and I really want to go. Could you meet me there at seven o'clock?"

"Sure," agreed Verona. "See you there."

Soon after they found their seats in the theater, Addie noticed five senior boys coming in who greeted her, smiled, and sat down beside her. She didn't know all of them, but she did recognize the boy sitting next to her. He was Rick Jones, a tall popular athlete. They were well into the feature presentation when Addie felt Rick's arm on the back of her chair.

His arms are so long he probably is resting one there while he gets something from his pocket, thought an amused Addie

But she was wrong. Rick's arm circled around the collar of her coat and rested on her shoulder.

Addie momentarily panicked. She was angry and mortified. She wanted to stand and lecture Rick vociferously, but instead, she took his arm with her left hand and brought it firmly down on his lap. Not a word was spoken, but Addie's grim demeanor left Rick miffed. As the leader of the pack, he motioned the other boys to leave, leading them down front where they dangled their long legs over the empty seats in the next row.

After the movie Addie and Verona left the theater hurriedly. When out of earshot of the general public, Addie exploded, "Verona, I should never have been a teacher. My classes haven't been worth a 'tinker's damn' all month. They don't listen or do their assignments—well, some do, but not very carefully. They look bored, act bored, and they are making me bored. I became a teacher to make a difference in young lives, but they're making a difference in mine, and it's not a good one."

"Lighten up, Addie," said Verona quickly as she took her arm and led her in a quicker walking pace. "Don't you remember you were feeling that way once before?"

Not listening, Addie interrupted, "And the fiasco I had to endure tonight."

Verona laughed. "It's okay. You'll be fine tomorrow. You're just having a 'spring teacher crash.'"

When they came to the gate to Addie's house, Verona gave her friend a quick hug and repeated, "Tomorrow you'll be fine. Remember, this is just a temporary 'teacher crash.' By the way, I coined that term just now—*teacher crash*. Do you like it?"

Maybe it will be funnier tomorrow, thought Addie as she managed a weak smile and said good night.

Verona and Jim's wedding day came on the heels of the end of the school year. Everyone was tired and drawn, except for Verona, who sparkled with anticipation and happiness.

On the Friday night before the wedding, Addie stopped at Ben's house. "I really need to talk," she explained.

He motioned her to the couch and sat beside her. "What's wrong, Addie?"

"It's the wedding. I hate even going to it, much less being a bridesmaid."

"Really? I thought women enjoyed that stuff," said Ben. "I thought it was probably a carryover from dressing up when you were a little girl."

She couldn't even laugh at Ben's analogy.

"Jim's a number 1 loser," she said, sitting up straight. "And he won't make her happy. She's vulnerable, and he thinks only of one thing, himself. You know that's true, Ben. I tried to talk to her about thinking it over longer, but she won't listen. She said she's never had a guy really love her before and that Jim is her prince." Softly, Addie added, "I'm afraid for her."

Ben put his arm around her and pulled her toward him. She nestled in the crook of his arm and was comforted by knowing that he was listening to her and understanding.

"Addie," he said, "even if you are correct, which I don't think you are, you're acting just like the sparrow that was trying to hold up the sky all by itself." He took her hands and said quietly, "'One does what one can.' You've done that, Addie. You've done all you can. Now you have to let go."

She sat quietly for a minute, absorbing his thoughts before asking, "Why are you always so smart and intuitive?"

"Because I go through some of those same feelings myself, Addie, when you start dating losers. Which you have a real talent for." His voice trailed as he reminisced, "Especially that last one, the nearsighted ophthalmologist."

"It took us both a while to realize we weren't seeing eye to eye," she quipped.

"I seem to sit on the sidelines, and I don't know why. I worry. I wonder, I wonder—what if she doesn't come back? What if she marries one of them?"

She had no answer, but sat quietly weighing his words, wondering why he didn't try to stop her foolish romances if he cared for her. She tried to get up, but he pulled her back and kissed her. It was a long, urgent kiss, not the consoling, comforting one she would have expected from Ben.

Noting her reaction, he apologized. "I'm sorry, Addie. I was just visualizing our walk down the aisle tomorrow, and I imagined that someday…"

"Someday, what?"

He didn't respond.

She waited.

Finally he said with such serious, formal tones that she wondered if he had rehearsed the words, "Addie, you must know I have feelings for you. I enjoy being with you, and I think our friendship is strong because we've always had good talks, even on topics that we differ on, like religion. I know that we've talked a lot in generalities about it and agreed that neither of us would marry outside our faith, but all this wedding business has me wondering what we would do if we should ever consider marriage. Would either of us reconsider and change faiths? I think it's a conundrum because I can't see a satisfactory solution. What do you think?"

"I don't know," answered Addie, rising from the sofa and getting ready to leave. "But I don't see God directing traffic up there and saying, 'Catholics to the East, Lutherans to the West.'"

She chuckled, adding, "He has enough to do separating all the Lutherans, the ALC, LFC, Missouri Synod, Wisconsin Synod…"

As Ben watched her arms gesture wildly while naming the groups, he began to laugh. He laughed so hard he had trouble telling her he would pick her up at six o'clock for the groom's dinner.

As Addie left, she agonized. I botched it, she thought. He wanted a long, serious conversation, but I just didn't know what to say, so I just gave him a lot of "fluff."

Addie wore her lavender suit to the dinner. She had combed her hair in an upsweep, a change that seemed to draw more attention to her blue eyes and flawless skin.

"You look gorgeous," he said as he opened the car door.

"You don't look so bad yourself," she responded, admiring his new, dark-brown suit, but somehow missing the familiar tweed look that was really Ben. Verona's mother introduced herself to Addie at the party.

"I'm so happy for Verona," she said, smiling at Addie. "Jim seems like such a fine young man. I couldn't be happier."

Addie forced a smile, then introduced her to Ben, who drew her into a conversation as only Ben could. She admired his ability to converse so easily and make people feel comfortable. Her feelings for him had steadily increased in intensity, and at times, she felt that his were doing the same. Often she felt that they were both walking around in a fog, unsure of what was ahead and, therefore, afraid to commit.

The dinner broke up quite early as the rehearsal would be on the following morning and the wedding would take place that evening. Ben walked her to her door. To Addie's surprise, he put his hands squarely on her shoulders and said, "I want us to have a pact."

"Sounds serious. What do you have in mind?" she asked, looking up at him.

"Neither of us will approach marriage without informing the other first."

She looked at him with curiosity, but answered, "Fine! It's an idea. I like it."

He looked down as if he were unsure of what should happen next. Finally he kissed her on the cheek, said, "Good night, dear Addie," and left.

The next evening, as she walked down the aisle in the wedding procession, Addie smiled at Ben as he joined her. He cut a dashing figure, wearing a white shirt, a black bow tie, and a black tuxedo that Addie knew he detested. A pink boutonniere in his lapel matched the pastel pink of Addie's off-the-shoulder dress with a bouffant chiffon skirt. For a fleeting moment, she wondered if any of his thoughts of the night before were present now, for she still felt a glow, remembering his kiss.

"I think we look pretty sharp," said Ben, winking at her.

"Watch out for my skirt. It's wide and treacherous."

"Oh, ye of little faith," he retorted.

Hearing the audience rise, they both turned to watch Verona. *She's more beautiful than ever*, thought Addie, as her friend stepped forward gracefully to claim her prince.

Addie spent a busy summer working at the Whitford Bank. She missed Ben but did not expect him to come to Whitford to visit. His letters described increasing responsibilities for community summer projects as well as numerous planning sessions with Rotary International. She wanted to tell her folks about the religious differences, but she put it off until the night before she was to return to Roseland.

"Addie, I can't approve of the relationship because if you marry you'll have too many problems," responded her father.

Agreeing, her mother added, "And you'll soon find someone else… I know you will."

Driving back to Roseland after a busy summer working at the grocery store, Addie was completely surprised to see a billboard picture of Ben with the caption, "Ben O'Reilly for Mayor—A Mayor who will care."

She knew that Ben would run for the office eventually, but she also knew he had no plans to run until Charley Stone decided to quit.

She couldn't wait to talk to someone about it, but she didn't have to wait long. Her landlady, Mrs. Hendrickson, greeted her with, "Addie, did you know about Mr. Stone? He has cancer and isn't expected to live very long. It is so sad. And did you know that Ben is running for the office? He's a friend of yours, isn't he?"

"Yes, we're good friends," she said as she rested her suitcase on the bottom rung of the stairway to her room.

"Well, I hope he wins. I don't think much of his opponent. That guy always wants to be a 'big shot.' But you know, he's got 'big shot' friends who can help him get in. It's all politics." Addie started up the stairs again but stopped quickly when she heard Mrs. Henderson say, "The papers are full of stories about teachers in larger towns who want more money. The articles are making people around here talk, too. They think you teachers get plenty of money for nine month's work." She said, "Who else gets three month's vacation? They say your days are short, but I tell them that I know that you work 'til midnight some nights correcting all those papers." She paused, then concluded, "With the town talking that way, maybe you can't be a lot of help to Ben, but maybe I'm wrong."

"More likely you're right," said Addie as she grabbed her suitcase and went quickly to her room upstairs to call Ben. He apologized for not writing but said life had been a whirlwind when Charley got sick and begged him to run in his place.

"I meant to write you about it," he said. "My opponent isn't really a strong candidate, but I'm sure he'll have some organizational support from groups he belongs to, and he's quite active community-wise."

"I hope you win, Ben, and so does Mrs. Hendrickson."

When she mentioned Mrs. Hendrickson's comments about town talk regarding teachers, Ben questioned the importance of the issue.

"I think the media is just stirring unrest," he said. "I wasn't aware of great dissatisfaction with salaries here, were you?"

"Not really, but I don't think we're progressive enough to see what's happening."

"What does that mean?"

"Well, there is a teacher shortage," said Addie, "and it will get worse unless we do something about it. We don't have enough qualified people entering the profession. Well, why should they start at thirty-five hundred dollars when they can make more money down the road? The world is changing, and the teaching profession is lagging behind."

"I agree. But tell me, can you justify the three months off? That's a long vacation."

"I don't think it should be all vacation. Teachers need time to refuel, but they could also go back to school and/or conventions and workshops to get more educational ideas that will help them become better teachers."

"On thirty-five hundred a year?"

"Exactly, Mr. Mayor. You perceive the problem well, and you will have my vote."

"I'm glad you're back."

"Likewise, Mr. Mayor."

He laughed and said goodbye.

The months up until the November election were busy. Addie did not actively campaign, but she helped by counting flyers and doing other work behind the scenes.

The Roseland Teachers Association invited Ben to speak at one of their meetings. He accepted.

The president introduced Ben as a "Friend of Education." As he approached the podium, Addie noticed that he didn't have any notes.

"Thank you for that introduction," said Ben. "I'd like to begin by telling you that I'll always be a friend to education because education has always been a friend to me. I really don't know what life would have been like for me without the schooling I've had, without the teachers I've had right here at Roseland, both nuns and public school teachers, who cared enough to motivate me to go further and do better.

"Education has also given me added dimensions to living by introducing me to Keats and Shelly, Mozart and Beethoven, and Picasso and Rembrandt. I had the opportunity to explore all of these areas even further at St. John's University.

"Yes, I'm a friend of education. If I'm elected mayor, I may not always agree with you on every stand you take, but you can be assured I'll do my best for the people of this town, and education will not be left out."

As the applause thundered, Addie joined the line to congratulate him.

Election night was long and cold with a hint of snow in the air. Ben invited Addie, along with a few friends who had campaigned hard for him, to his place to wait for the election returns. In the beginning, Ben held a strong lead, but by six o'clock, his lead was wavering and results were in doubt. Addie leaned back in Ben's comfortable recliner. Excited as she was, she closed her eyes during a lengthy commercial and inadvertently dozed off.

Ben awakened her at 2:00 a.m. She had slept so hard she had trouble realizing she was still at Ben's house. She pushed off the blanket he had put over her, looked around and saw that everyone had left.

"I hated to wake you," said Ben, folding the blanket. Teasingly, he added, "but I can't risk losing my reputation before I'm even sworn in."

"You won, Ben!" she screamed as she quickly pulled herself out of the recliner.

"This will be the biggest hug you've ever had," she said as she held out her arms to him.

"You're a mad hugger," he said embracing her. "I can't really believe that you're Norwegian and Lutheran at that."

As they walked to her car, she stopped to do a mock curtsy. "Whatever my pedigree, Mr. Mayor, I will serve you as best I can."

"Good," Ben said, laughing. "Good decision, Addie." He shut the car door but leaned through the open window as he added, "And smart too."

She responded by hitting the gas pedal hard which created such a blast that the lights went on next door. Addie regretted her action because now, she thought, Mrs. Hugelstad, Ben's neighbor, could begin her reports on the new mayor and his friends.

The next morning, the Roseland faculty was exuberant over Ben's victory. Verona looked especially joyous. She had always admired Ben and told him she would do everything possible to help. She had voted with five elderly friends who, Addie was sure, had been properly coached. Later, when Jim came with a group of women teachers, Addie wondered if Verona's marriage was in trouble. It seemed as though the couple's lifestyle was becoming more separate than together.

Maybe she just gets tired of listening to him talk, thought Addie, but she worried about her and didn't dare ask.

A new school year was always an exciting time for Addie. She thought of it as a time for new challenges, also a time for teachers to come back refreshed and ready to "give all they had" in order to accomplish good things in students' lives.

Teaching was never static. It was full of peaks and valleys, and no two days were the same. The climate of each class was different. As a teacher, she must deal with the learning experiences a student has had to this point and, from these experiences, try to expand horizons.

Seeing old colleagues and meeting new ones was also a part of the fall excitement. To everyone's dismay, Larry Jones, the assistant coach, had resigned to accept a position in Montana. Addie knew his dry humor would be missed, especially since his replacement seemed so quiet.

Sharon Middleton had also resigned her music position during the summer. A letter to Addie disclosed that at Christmastime she would marry her hometown boyfriend of three years. Replacing her was Estelle Jones, a young black music teacher from Minneapolis. She was a very tall, thin, strikingly beautiful woman with dark hair pulled back over her ears, serving to emphasize the classic gold or silver hoop earrings that she usually wore. She dressed well and had a beautiful contralto voice that reminded older folks of Marian Anderson. Addie never tired of watching Estelle's expressive conducting and listening to her chorus as they sang difficult numbers so beautifully. Standing room only soon became the norm at her concerts. Her high school band was equally good, and the community was extremely proud of both groups.

Estelle decided to rent a room at Mrs. Hendrickson's house, where she and Addie became good friends. Estelle returned to Minneapolis most weekends, but when she stayed at Roseland, she enjoyed the friendliness of the people who gathered at Ben's home.

One Friday night they all decided to go to a local service club for dinner. Estelle decided to stay home.

"I'm not feeling hungry enough," she said.

"They have great salads there," said Addie. "Come with us. It will be fun."

"No, I'm going home," Estelle insisted. "You go ahead and enjoy the evening."

Trailing her to her car, Addie pleaded with her friend, but again and again met with refusal.

Finally Estelle exploded. "You don't get it, Addie. You think everything is easy for black people in a neat little town like this, don't you? Well, it isn't. They wouldn't let me into that club. They can't because they're affiliated with a national group that prohibits it. That's what it's like for us. My band, my chorus and I make music together, and at these times, we are in complete unity, as if we are all one color, race, and creed. We all work together, just like your sparrows, but when I turn around and face the audience, my outer skin is not acceptable."

Seeing Addie upset, she put her arm around her and said gently, "Please don't spoil it for the others by mentioning this dilemma. Just say that I had a headache. Believe me, I do." She laughed as she noted, "I think that people of my color take more aspirin than anyone else."

Coming into the club, Addie was greeted warmly. Listening to the others rave about the chef, she ordered a prime rib dinner. When it came, she could think only of Estelle.

"Why aren't you eating?" asked Ben.

"I'm not hungry," she answered.

The service club episode awakened Addie to the racial injustices that were still occurring, even in the small town of Roseland. Estelle's skilled musicianship and teaching abilities gained wide acclaim, and she was nominated for state music teacher of the year. When she didn't win, Addie strongly suspected it was because of her color. Again, Addie kept her feelings to herself, but she scrutinized the papers for news about racial inequalities, Martin Luther King, and the marches in the South.

An advertisement placed by Tuskegee Institute in a national magazine finally transported Addie from passivism to activism. It stated that people who were interested in helping disadvantaged children in the South should answer the advertisement and find out how they could volunteer to join the fight for equality. Addie immediately read it to Estelle.

"We can both help during the summer," Addie said. "Let's think about it a little first," responded Estelle. "Really? What's to think about?"

"You've never been South, and you don't know what to expect. I'm afraid for you."

You're a sensitive person and a culture change is not easy for anyone to accept. Believe me, I felt it when I moved North. To add to it, the South is in a lot of turmoil with integration problems causing riots and—"

"But don't you see?" interrupted Addie. "We have a golden opportunity to be 'downfront' as history changes."

"People get hurt 'down-front', Addie."

"I know, but I can get hurt crossing the street outside. That doesn't mean I'm going to stay on this side forever. We might have a chance to hold up a little of their sky. Just think of the possibilities."

"You are indomitable!" exclaimed Estelle, but with a smile she added, "Okay. You win. Let's fly South."

Chapter 5

SOUTHERN EXPOSURE

On a hot summer day in June 1966, Addie and Estelle left Interstate 65 to drive on back roads leading to Lowndes County, Alabama, where they would be volunteers. Addie was unaware that this summer experience would change her focus on life.

They met with officials of the Tuskegee Institute Community Education Program who repeated their philosophy that TICEP was meant to help treat injuries of the past and help children of the area. Blacks who accepted the program would contact TICEP and agree that volunteers involved in the program could stay with them in their homes and offer assistance.

On the evening of the third day of their trip, Addie pulled up to the house where they would spend the summer. It was a large wooden structure in need of both repair and paint. Addie stopped the car, looked at Estelle, and said, "Any second thoughts?"

"Not a one," answered Estelle as she grabbed her suitcase from the back seat. "Come on, Addie. This was your idea." She smiled at her and said, "And a darn good one."

As they walked up the wooden steps to the modest house, the door was opened by a short, wiry woman with skin the color of coffee and silver-colored hair pulled back over her head. "Praise the Lawd!" she called. "Y'all must be the teachers from Minnesota!"

Addie and Estelle nodded.

"Dey call me Miss Maribelle. Come in. Come on in, y'all, 'n meet my kinfolk. We's so glad ya heah." Miss Maribelle ushered them into a large kitchen, which housed wooden cupboards, a long wooden table and chairs, a gas cook stove, and a vintage refrigerator. A flowered linoleum, slightly cracked, covered the floors. Miss Maribelle's eyes twinkled with pride as she introduced Addie and Estelle to her granddaughter, Zelda, and Zelda's husband, Zach. Zelda was a tall, attractive woman with cinnamon-colored skin and dark brown hair. Zach, darker skinned, had a stocky build and pleasant countenance.

"Dey both work in the store, but dey took time off to welcome you," said Miss Maribelle.

Zelda smiled and said, "We're glad you're here."

"I hope you'll come and see the store," said Zach. "There's a lot that needs fixin', but someday, Zelda and I will get it done." He started to laugh as their daughter, Rebecca, who looked a lot like Zelda, came into the kitchen at breakneck speed. She was trying to hold back her twin daughters, Missy and Lucy, age two. Rebecca's husband, Josiah, worked in a city, one hundred miles away and was home only on weekends. During the week, the twins were often a handful because Zach and Zelda were busy at the store and Miss Maribelle's energy would waver.

The twins, Missy and Lucy, gave their own welcome by accepting Addie and Estelle's offer to hold them. As Addie felt the tiny dark arms winding around her neck, she experienced a wonderful feeling of contentment interrupted already by the thought of how difficult it might become to leave such precious little ones.

Addie and Estelle were overcome with the warmth of this family who seemed to cut through the fog of background differences. At ninety-five, Miss Maribelle still laughed easily and praised God constantly for protecting her and her family. "And please, Lord, keep our new friends safe, too," she said as she pointed in their direction. Then she broke into a chorus of "Sweet Jesus," accompanied by the rest of the family who harmonized and sang with conviction. That evening, Estelle and Addie, along with a few neighbors, joined the chorus, learning songs that had been handed down from past generations. They also listened to Miss Maribelle talk about her daughter, Zelda's mother, who had recently passed away from cancer, and of Miss Maribelle's grandmother, who had been a slave. She told how her grandmother had been "bidded off" at the auction block with bidders checking her body with utter disregard for human dignity.

Addie's tears came as she listened, but Estelle's face was immobile, as though she had heard it all before.

As they relaxed before bedtime in the small room they shared, Addie asked, "Weren't Miss Maribelle's stories disturbing? How could that happen?"

"It did happen," answered Estelle sharply. "You have to remember that your history books leave out a lot of what happened to our race in the past. Any reference to our treatment has a high-class gloss job, and if you peel off that protective covering, the reality can be shocking. But believe her story because that's the way it was."

Addie didn't sleep that night or the next. She had trouble with the culture shock she was experiencing, but adding historical shock was almost more than she could handle. Her thoughts also wandered to Ben. Their special times flooded her memory channel as she visualized him dressed in his gray tweed jacket and dark slacks welcoming the Friday night group to his home. She felt that her feelings for him were becoming increasingly stronger and wondered if his were the same. She told herself it was too early in a relationship to know, so she tried to drive it from her mind. She could not, however, dispel the feeling she was falling in love.

Sitting around the long kitchen table, Addie began working with eight neighborhood children who had learning problems. Reading was particularly troublesome. Some, like Carl, were suffering from learning disabilities while some just needed more individual attention.

Estelle often helped Zelda and Zach at the general store. Her father owned a grocery store in Minneapolis, and she was aware of problems that could arise in many areas of sales and management. She was also eager to help the young students who worked there, hoping that some of them could someday become successful entrepreneurs.

One of the students would sometimes sing as he worked. Estelle, impressed by his ability, began giving him vocal lessons. She felt that his rich baritone voice had possibilities.

"I'll leave some recordings for you to work with this winter," said Estelle, "and when I come back, you can perform them for me."

The young singer's face brightened. "You comin' back next year?"

"I wouldn't miss it," she answered. "Both Miss Carlson and I hope to return."

One day, Sheriff Barton, a black man whose full-bodied figure emanated strength and confidence, stopped by. Barton, a local son, had been sheriff for only one year, but he had already gained the respect of the community.

"Have you gotten to know Miss Maribelle, ma'am?" he asked.

"Not as well as we'd like," answered Addie.

"She's quite a lady," said Barton. "When she was young, she always wore heels, said her feet 'behaved' better in 'em. She even wore 'em when she hoed cotton. When I was small, I went by that field every day on my bike, and Miss Maribelle always looked so grand. I remember she had two good-lookin' skirts and tops she wore. We called her the 'dress-up lady.'"

Smiling, Sheriff Barton continued, "She was awful good to me and my brother. She'd stop us every time we passed her place on the way to the store, and she'd say, 'Boys, get me a small bag of sugar,' or whatever she needed. 'Here's an egg a piece to trade for a sweet treat for yourselves.' On our way back she'd ask, 'Now don't that make you feel trembleacious?' Well, I didn't know Miss Maribelle had made up that word, so I used it all the time. Whenever she asked me how I was feelin', I'd say, 'Real trembleacious.'"

The sheriff, realizing he was playing to a very appreciative audience, continued reminiscing. "She loved children, but she meant for us to be respectful and mind our manners." Laughing, he said, "I remember one time Mrs. Eliason's four screamin' kids got on Miss

Maribelle's one last nerve, and she told me, 'Mamas always love their children, but said they need to raise 'em so other folks love 'em too."

"She's had her share of tragedy," continued Barton. "She lost a daughter to cancer and her first husband died when he was only twenty-four."

"What happened?" asked Estelle.

Looking at his watch, the sheriff said, "I don' have time to tell the story now. I have a meeting in ten minutes, but ask Miss Maribelle. She'll tell you about it. I just stopped by to wish you a pleasant day. An', ma'am, we have three young men in our jail needin' help with their readin' 'n writin'. You got some time for 'em?"

"We do," said Addie. "How about tomorrow?"

"Any time after eight-thirty. We'd really appreciate it," he said.

"We'll be there at nine," offered Estelle.

Later that afternoon. Addie finished a session in the kitchen with neighborhood children who needed help in mastering basic skills. After dismissing the class, she joined Miss Maribelle and Estelle on the porch for a glass of lemonade.

"What are you discussing?" asked Addie.

Estelle smiled and said, "I was just asking Miss Maribelle about her first husband."

"Billy was a good-lookin' man!" exclaimed Miss Maribelle with a broad grin. "He had smooth, black skin like I'd never seen or felt before." She winked as she added, "He made me feel so trembleacious."

"He was a good man, too," she continued. "Though sometime' I'd upset him, and then he'd put his hands on his hips and say, 'Woman, if you wasn't so little, I'd have to beat you.'"

Addie gasped, "Did he?"

"No, oh no," answered Miss Maribelle quickly. "I'm proud to say my husband's never laid hands on me. No, no. Billy, my first husband, could take care of himself in a fight, but he was a gentleman at home."

"What happened to him?" asked Estelle warily. "Can you tell us?"

"Murdered," murmured Miss Maribelle. "But it ain' no pretty story. At the time it tore me up real bad, but I kin talk 'bout it now."

She paused to fill the lemonade glasses before describing the four white deputies who arrived at her house with carbine rifles pointed out the windows of their car.

"They asked for Billy, and I went to the field and got him," said Miss Maribelle. "I didn't know why they wanted him, and I don't think he did either. They told him they was taking him in for poachin'. Billy would shoot a possum, coon, or squirrel out-of-season so we could eat. Folks went to bed hungry in those days." She paused before reflecting, "Lots of 'em would poach, but they only came for my man."

"Why?" asked Addie.

"Maybe 'cuz Billy would speak up, thought he was as good as anyone else," answered Miss Maribelle proudly.

"What happened then, Miss Maribelle?" asked Estelle.

"They told him to git in their car, but my husband said he'd change his clothes first. 'Billy, you're gonna come with us right now,' said one of the men."

Smiling proudly, Miss Maribelle said, "But my husband just kept walking tall into the house. He stopped behind the closed screen door and called out, 'I'll change my clothes or go to hell.' He knew black people's lives was taken without cause, and he sure wasn't gonna git in their car and make it easy for them. In a few minutes, he came back out," she continued. "The men shouted, 'Come on, Billy. Get in.' But Billy said that he would ride his mule instead, knowing it was safer than getting in that car. Billy was a mighty brave man," continued Miss Maribelle. "And I was proud of what he said next. 'I'll ride my mule or go to hell,' he called." Softly, she added, "But then, I had to watch Billy ride off alone on his mule while the men pulled off in their car."

With a voice barely audible and a faraway look in her eyes, Miss Maribelle mused, "And that was the last time I saw my man alive. They shot him in the back before he made it to town, and they left him in the ditch like he was a dog. When his mule come back home alone, I knowed what happened. I just knowed... I loved that man." Miss Maribelle's voice trailed off and Addie quickly opened her purse for a handkerchief. She wanted to comfort this lady who had been through such a loss, but the words didn't seem to form—only tears as she looked into Miss Maribelle's eyes and whispered, "I'm so sorry. I don't know how you found the strength."

"Jesus is my strength," interrupted Miss Maribelle, "and He's blessed me with lovin' kinfolk and sweet friends like you…and he gave me another man after that who was a fine man too, but God took him home when he was only forty-five. He fell out hoein' cotton on a blisterin' hot day."

Looking at Estelle, Addie noticed her pursed lips and the intense expression on her face—a countenance Estelle exposed only when severely shaken.

"Do you mind if I ask your age?" inquired Addie.

"No," she answered. "I'm ninety-five, and I'm in God's hands now, on His time. I live with Jesus every day, and it will be wonderful to see Him face-to-face. But when I think about leavin' here, it makes me a little afraid, not of heaven, but a person needs to die to get there."

Miss Maribelle smiled, and her eyes twinkled as she leaned forward and said secretively, "But then I jist say to myself, 'Well, if you don't wanna leave here, you ought not to have come.'"

Laughing, she pushed back wisps of long silver hair and said, "I hear the young ones." She left the room humming the chorus of 'Sweet Jesus.'"

That night, before turning out the lights in their bedroom, Addie said, "What a life Miss Maribelle has had. Can't you just see her in the fields dressed like she should be at a party? She must have washed clothes every night. I just can't understand her."

"Remember, her grandmother was a slave, and Miss Maribelle probably visited her. Maybe she was so impressed with the beautiful clothes of the plantation ladies that she just wanted to grab a little part of that elegance for her own life…whether it fit or not."

"Do you really think so?"

"I don't know. It is just a figment of my imagination, but I do wonder why, but I'm wondering about a lot of things."

"Such as?"

"Well, what Miss Maribelle would be like if she were our age... what she would be doing...what she would have accomplished...and to go a step further...what she would be like if she had been born with white skin?"

I should have waited until morning to ask her what she was wondering, thought Addie as she mulled Estelle's comments over and over in her mind, especially the picture of Miss Maribelle as a white woman. When sleep did not come, she extended her roommate's psychological musings to a more personal level. What if she and Estelle could exchange skin colors? What would be the changes? Could they live with them?

The time Addie and Estelle spent at the jail proved to be difficult. Seeing Zane Smith, a seventeen-year-old in jail charged with murder, and the others from the ages of sixteen to twenty charged with aggravated robbery and assault, was heartbreaking for the two young volunteers.

"When is Zane's trial?" asked Addie.

"Not for another six months at least," said the sheriff. "The law seems to be puttin' it off. Zane says he is innocent, but they seem to be looking for more evidence."

"Do you think he killed the man?" asked Addie.

"I don't think so, but when it involves a white man and a black man, it's hard to tell what can happen. I'm sorry to say that a black man could be picked at random to pay for a crime. I've seen it happen too often."

Addie worried about Zane's future. She found him to be a bright student with talent in writing. His essays on the virtues of democracy and the concept of freedom had exceptional content but poor grammar. She felt deep empathy for this young man who found himself in such an untenable situation. He never talked about his case to her, but the maturity of his feelings, as expressed in his writing, impressed Addie so much that she found it difficult to believe him guilty.

At times, her discussions with him reached a personal level. She knew he had been raised by his grandmother and that she had died recently, leaving Zane alone to face the charge of murder.

"What happened to your father?" she asked one day.

"I don't know. He left and didn't ever stop by. They tell me he passed."

"And your mother?"

"She passed when I was born. I lived with my grandmama."

"And you've been alone since she died?"

"Yup."

"Are you afraid?"

"Nope."

"Would you tell me if you were?"

His eyes met hers as though he were questioning the validity of her inquiry. He smiled and gave a slightly affirmative nod, then teasingly changed his response to "maybe."

After her sessions with him, it was hard for her to see the gate close on Zane's freedom. She wondered what would happen to him. Would he still be in jail when she returned next summer? How much more could this young man tolerate before breaking? She posed the question to Sheriff Barton who told her not to worry, that he would write if anything serious developed before her return.

The summer went quickly. It was the middle of August. Both women had tried not to think of the summer ending. They had begun to realize that their bonds with Miss Maribelle, her family, and the students they served were stronger than they could ever have imagined. As Addie read to the twins and tucked them in, she worried about their future. She wondered how much of their boundless love and trust could remain as the country struggled with racial inequality.

But her greatest worry was for Zane. On her last visit, she emphasized being strong and looking toward a brighter future.

"I pray for you every night, Zane," she said. "And I'm going to try my very hardest to help hold up the sky for you. I've told Sheriff Barton that I'll be sending you books to read. Use this time to enjoy reading and to nurture your mind…and I'll see you next June."

"I will. Thanks, Ms. Carlson."

Tears welled as she said goodbye and again promised to return.

Too soon, it was time to leave. They planned a farewell dinner at Selma, but Josiah cautioned Addie against going. "It might be risky," he said. "Some don't like to see white folks together with black ones."

But Addie wouldn't hear of canceling the trip. "I'm not afraid," she said.

"I'll drive with you," said Zach.

Toward the end of August, they left for Selma. Addie had Estelle, Miss Maribelle, Zach, and Zelda in her car, while Rebecca and the twins drove with Josiah.

The evening meal, enjoyed at a Baptist church celebration, was without incident. No staring eyes posed any alarm as they laughed and enjoyed the evening to the fullest. It was agreed that Addie and Estelle would write during the school year and return the following summer.

As they drove home, Estelle commented on the beauty of the evening. The stars were bright. The night was peaceful. It had been a wonderful day, followed by a perfect evening—all summed up by Miss Maribelle's words, "It makes me feel trembleacious."

"I really think conditions will improve for us," said Zelda. "The freedom marches and TICEP are both beginning to make a difference."

"I hope they make a difference for Zane," said Zach. "I don't think he can stand staying in jail for years while he waits for his trial. That happens sometimes here, you know."

"We'll pray him out," called Miss Maribelle from the back seat. "Trust the Lord."

Deciding on a back road that would avoid heavy traffic, Addie took the next turn. Suddenly a car zooming out of nowhere came from behind at breakneck speed, hitting her on the driver's side. Addie screamed and hit the brakes hard, causing her head to hit the steering wheel and one of her legs to twist and slam against the iron of the car's interior. Zach, who was in the front seat, lurched forward and hit his head on the windshield. Estelle, Zelda, and Miss Maribelle were in the back seat, seemingly unscathed, but Addie moaned with pain. Zach wiped blood from his face as the other car sped away.

Addie awoke in the hospital at Selma. Her head was still sore, but a concussion had been ruled out. Her leg was broken and she was in a leg cast that reached just above her left knee. She wondered how she could ever get home.

Zach had been released from the hospital after having some stitches taken in his forehead.

No one else had been hurt.

"They want to keep you for a few days to be sure you can manage your crutches," said Estelle. "I'll drive your car home and you, of course, will fly."

"But what about the steps to the plane?"

"They have enclosed tunnels now, so you'll be all right. I called Ben and told him I would put you on the plane to Montgomery. He's planning to meet you in Minneapolis to drive you home. I also called Mrs. Hendrickson, and she's already moved you to the downstairs bedroom in her house. She says she'll take good care of you, and you know she will."

Addie was overcome with the help that people were offering. She held back a smile as she thought of Mrs. Hendrickson, who would be more than helpful and would tell the town about each step in her progress toward recovery.

She's a dear lady, thought Addie, but in the same breath, she asked God to get her back to school quickly.

The plane was an hour late getting into Minneapolis. Calling for a wheelchair to transport her, she held the crutches on her lap. When almost to the baggage center, she spied Ben, whose smile radiated as he bent down to give her a hug. After waiting almost a half hour for her suitcase, which was easy to recognize because of the colorful yarn Estelle had attached to the handle, Ben grabbed it and took it to his car, then returned for Addie. She laughed at his carefulness in helping her out of the chair and guiding each step.

"I'm not a china doll," she said. "I won't crack, Ben. I'll bet no one could crack this cast, not even you."

"One does what one can," teased Ben, causing Addie to think again of Zane and the philosophy of the sparrow. *Someone needs to come forward and help him*, she agonized silently. Suddenly she realized that Ben had been talking to her and she hadn't been listening.

"Come back, Addie," he said.

"I'm sorry," she answered, smiling. "I know I have to stop thinking about the summer."

But she couldn't break away from thoughts of Zane pacing the floor of his narrow jail cell. She also thought of the children in her class who needed more help with basic skills. "It's so hard to let go," she murmured as she focused on the twins, remembering especially the feeling of their soft, velvety skin pressing against her face.

Brushing aside an errant tear, she forced herself into the present, a new term at Roseland High.

Addie missed the fall workshop activities but was on deck the first day of school. By noon, every inch of her cast was covered with student signatures, and "Miss Carlson needs help" became the password of the day.

I need to fight for my independence, thought Addie. *They're too helpful, and they're driving me crazy. Soon they'll take over my class.*

"Look," she told them. "I have no pain. My mobility is not good right now, but my cast is only temporary. It will come off in a month, so instead of worrying about me, let's think for a minute about the people I left back in Alabama."

The class was quietly respectful as Addie continued. "Miss Jones and I have an idea we would really like you to consider. We're wondering if you could help us raise money for books for their library. Teachers and students could provide coffee and bars or cookies for the teacher's lounge every day. There are sixty teachers in the building and not everyone will stop for coffee, of course, but we could probably make a sizeable amount of money with this project if we charge 25 cents for a treat and coffee."

The class was enthusiastic and approximately half the class signed their names as providers.

"Explain the project and check with your parents," said Addie. "If you change your mind after talking to them, just erase your name from the list."

Addie received letters of protest, citing activities right in their own school that needed funding, but sixteen parents offered to help. With fifteen teachers also joining the project, each of the thirty-one volunteers was responsible for baking cookies or bars once a month.

Approximately half of the faculty purchased treats daily, providing almost $225 a month.

Entering the lounge one day, she smiled as she noticed a sign above the coffee pot. Black letters on white tag board read "Remember the Sparrow."

This is a great way to begin a new school year at Roseland, thought Addie as the project began. Not even the cast on her leg could dull her enthusiasm.

The treats were a hit with the faculty, and the students caught the spirit of the efforts to help buy books for the library in Alabama. The speech class surprised Addie by announcing they were holding an auction at school and were busy collecting items for the event. One student, disappointed in the results, complained to Addie. She thanked him for his efforts and said that future sales would get better as more people understood the needs of the students in the South.

For Addie, the school year whirled by. As April approached, she was delighted to find that lounge treats had netted over a thousand dollars.

Both Addie and Estelle were eager to make a return visit to their friends in Lowndes County, but plans were interrupted when Addie received a surprise call from her father.

"I need to talk to you about your mother."

"What's wrong?"

He hesitated as though he could not spurt out the words. "She's mixed up, Addie. She leaves the house at night sometimes. I can't sleep for worrying about her. She thinks her folks are alive. You'll see at Easter, but I didn't want you to be unaware of what's happening."

Easter was in two weeks, but it seemed like two months to Addie before she could arrive home.

"Hi, Addie," said her mother, welcoming her with a hug. "How's college going? Have you decided what you'll do?"

Surprised, Addie looked at her mother and saw the same wonderful smile and earnest concern she had always shown.

"Yes, I'm teaching now, Mom," she responded. "I decided to go into teaching."

"Good," said her mother. "I was hoping you would do that. I never did want you to go into nursing."

Addie looked at her father. "Dad," she said, "you can't be alone. I'll come home for the summer."

"That would be good. I can't watch her while I put in the crops and harvest them. But you have plans to go to Alabama, and that's important too."

"We'll work out something. The thing is, you may need help all year."

"We can't afford it. We'll make it, Addie. Don't worry."

"Yes, we'll make it," comforted Addie, but she worried about his health and endurance.

Chapter 6

DECISIONS

Arriving back in Roseland on Easter Monday, Addie quickly dialed Ben's number. "I'm glad you're back. I have two tall glasses of lemonade waiting for us."

"Sounds great."

Since they both needed to walk, Ben suggested starting from their own houses, meeting somewhere between, and continuing together back to Ben's house. Smiling, Addie agreed, knowing his tall, lean frame could cover twice as much territory as she could in the allotted time. She had always admired his physique, but she also liked the scholarly look that his black hornrimmed glasses provided. Addie knew her attraction to him was not only physical because, as she told Verona, she was also completely captivated by his relaxed manner, quick mind, and power of communication. The irony, she thought, was that they didn't seem able to communicate when it came to sharing their feelings about each other.

As she walked, she worried about the decision she would have to make, whether to leave Roseland or find some way she could stay. She could not stop the ache that surfaced when she thought of not being able to sit with Ben and discuss whatever topics might emerge. She smiled, remembering evenings at Ben's house with friends who always teased him about the tweed jackets he liked to wear. They were her favorites as well.

At the end of each block, she paused as though to plant each scene in her memory. Finally breaking her train of thought, she looked up to see Ben a block away. In his hand was a red rose he had received from the new floral shop, which he presented to her with an effusive bow.

As they walked toward Ben's house, he asked about her folks.

"My mother is requiring more care," she answered. "It was hard for me to see her this way. She doesn't eat much, and she's losing weight. She's pale and doesn't sleep well. I want to talk to her, but I can't reach her. I want to ask her how she is and if she's scared. She needs to be reassured that we won't leave her, that we'll always be able to help her."

"So what will you do?"

"I don't know," she answered. "I wish someone could tell me."

She waited for a comment, but when it didn't come she continued, "I don't think Dad can handle her alone either this summer or next year, and there doesn't seem to be much the doctors can do. Wouldn't you think they could do more?"

Ben replied they were trying, but the brain is pretty much a mystery. "What matters now," he said, putting his arm around her shoulder, "is to see that she has good care and that's what you're giving her."

Not responding to his statement, she continued softly, "She keeps emptying and refilling her purse, she asks the same inane questions all the time and repeats silly statements again and again. Sometimes, I'm so short with this dear, sweet lady who has given me so much love, and now, she can hardly remember the words to 'Jesus Loves Me.' I feel so terrible."

Holding back tears, she added sharply, "It's cruel and unfair to all of us, and I'm also concerned about my father who seems to be placating her by sharing her fantasies."

"He's doing what he's always done, Addie. He's trying to make her happy, but in a different way because now he needs to enter her world."

She looked at him, admiring his assessment of the situation. He always seemed to put things in just the right perspective. Why couldn't she do the same?

"I guess you're right," she said. "And I have to decide whether to get a job near Whitford or get a house and move them here. They don't want to move, and I must be a selfish, selfserving person because I can't seem to face the prospect of leaving Roseland. I love my job, and I don't want to leave my friends. And then there's Zane who is sitting in jail in Alabama. I promised him I'd be back this summer to help. Now I can't. I don't know what to do."

He took her hand, and they walked without speaking. His presence seemed to act as a momentary buffer against forces that were threatening.

Nearing his house, Ben broke the silence. "I wish I could help make your decision. I can't do that, but I'll support whatever you decide. You know that."

Impulsively, Addie stopped and grasped both his hands, saying, "I don't want to leave you."

He kissed her gently and said, "I don't want you to leave either. God knows I don't want you to leave. I need you in my life."

As he drove Addie home, neither spoke much. Thoughts Addie had harbored for a long time resurfaced. If she turned Catholic, could she accept the differences? When she entertained the "yes" answer, it seemed to waver as she thought of giving up the Lutheran beliefs. And where would the children fit in? Often, after watching Ben play a fatherly role with the neighborhood children, she felt her decision should be a "yes," and after spending so many happy times with Ben, the "yes" would be accentuated. But then it seemed to falter as her father joined her at Sunday morning services.

The next day, Addie met Estelle for lunch at the cafeteria. After hearing about the weekend, Estelle was silent, seemingly in deep thought. Finally she said, "It looks like you are going to have to make a decision soon. You shouldn't worry about it. Whatever you decide will be in God's hands."

"You're right," agreed Addie. "And one of the decisions will have to be about Alabama. I'm really concerned about not returning there. I promised Zane I'd be back."

"I have friends from Minneapolis who are eager to join us. We'll all do our best for Zane and we'll call you for your input. It will work out fine."

As she rose to leave, Estelle teased, "I s'pose you'll ask me to comment on the Addie, Ben saga too. Well, I'm sorry, but I don't have an answer for that one. I know that only God can handle the two of you."

Addie laughed as she watched her leave, realizing Estelle was both wise and thoughtful.

Her decision to stay or to leave Roseland had to be made soon and alone.

Her sleep patterns became erratic. On sleepless nights, she made lists of positives and negatives related to whichever course she was considering. She thought of the impact her decision might have on people she cared for, the consequences of her choices and, finally, her own desires.

After much soul-searching and prayer, she rose one morning with a great sense of relief.

She had made her decision, and in her mind, it was right.

In May, Addie handed her letter of resignation to the Roseland School Board. The last gathering at Ben's place proved difficult as she said goodbye to everyone except Verona, who was at home ill. Leaving Ben was the hardest, but they both agreed that the separation would either bring them closer or bring closure to the relationship, and they would have to accept the outcome.

She would miss the long hikes in the woods, picnics in the park, bowling on a team, and dancing at the club, but she knew she needed to be near her father who suffered as he watched his wife's decline in both physical strength and mental functions.

Addie interviewed for a position at Miller, a town smaller than Roseland but only twenty miles east of Whitford. The superintendent, Mr. Kelly, surprised her by saying, "I noticed you have a degree in music, also. We have a part-time elementary music position open. Would you consider half-time English and half-time music?"

Addie laughed and said, "No, I don't think so."

He told her to think about it. "Fewer themes to correct," he joked. Addie phoned Estelle for advice.

"Take it, Addie," said Estelle. "You'll love it. The superintendent is right. It will be a welcome change from correcting themes and other papers, and you'll love the children."

Addie thought of Mr. Johnson, her college vocal teacher who had motivated her to earn a degree in both English and music. "You have a good background in piano and a wonderful voice," he had said. "You would enjoy teaching music."

Addie decided to sign the contract.

In June, Addie received a letter from Ben. Written in his usual scholarly style, he wrote about his difficulty in accepting the fact she was leaving.

"As we go through this life," he wrote, "there are few people that we ever want to cling to tenaciously. You are one of these people, Addie, that I can't 'let go.' As a couple, we are fortunate enough to almost see into each other's souls and form an indestructible bond. Time and distance may dull it, but I feel that it will always be sustained." He closed by saying, "I want you and need you beside me, Addie. It is too hard to let you go."

The letter touched her deeply. She missed him. Her feelings, too, were becoming more intense, but she still wondered if their Catholic-Protestant relationship could survive with both of them so dedicated to keeping religion on different channels. She wondered if she would be able to switch. Or would he? Or would neither of them?

She meant to answer Ben's letter but could never find the words. Her own thoughts were too mixed up. She read and reread his letter, visualizing him sitting in the brown chair that he always occupied, checking his letter for any errors. She shoved the letter aside and vowed to answer when her thoughts became clearer.

When they hadn't cleared after two weeks, she decided to answer it anyway. She began with news about her mother's health, then wrote that Verona had invited her to come for the weekend, and she hoped to see him then.

She closed by writing, "Ben, your letter touched me so deeply. I feel I could send the same words right back to you, for you are, I am certain, the closest to a soul mate that I will ever encounter on this earth. I miss you greatly and hope and pray we can weather this separation."

Addie arrived in Roseland at five o'clock Saturday evening. She drove past the elementary school and turned the corner. Verona had a small white house with a classic picket fence and petunias and pansies lining the walkway.

Verona was mowing the lawn. Addie wondered why Jim wasn't doing it, but she decided to put aside her mental attacks on him.

Who knows? she thought. *Maybe he has a job.* She smiled at the possibility, since being industrious had never been one of Jim's stronger points.

Verona shut off the mower and ran to embrace her friend. "I'm so glad you're here. It's only been a month, but I've missed you like ten."

Addie laughed. "We'll get caught up," she answered, as she stepped back to take a good look at her friend who, she thought, looked tired.

As they entered the house, Verona led her to the kitchen and seated her at a small white table that was already set for tea. The rose trim on the teapot and coffee server matched the trim of the border on the off-white wallpaper.

"Your house looks so lovely," said Addie. "I should have you come to Whitford and help me."

"Well, I'm up for hire."

Addie looked at her quizzically. "What does that mean?"

"I'm looking for a new teaching job," said Verona as she placed a plate of snickerdoodle cookies in front of Addie.

A red flag arose in Addie's mind. She hoped her worries about Verona's marriage were not proving to be well-founded.

"I'm surprised," said Addie. "What about Jim?"

"How do they say it in the movies? He's history."

"What happened?"

"A lot," she answered, pausing and breathing deeply before continuing. "Everything fell apart the last two weeks of school. He never came home until midnight and said he was working late at school with some new program that would start up in the fall."

"You didn't believe him?" asked Addie as she took another cookie.

"I guess I trusted him, but I needed to talk to him. I hadn't had a chance to talk to him at home, so I decided to stop down at school just to talk."

Verona's voice broke and she took a sip of tea.

"I opened the door, calling, 'Jim, we need to talk,' but of course, I stopped talking when I saw them. He was kissing one of the school secretaries."

"What a shock," said Addie. "What did you do?"

"I shouted, 'I came to tell you I think I'm pregnant, but now, I hope to God I'm not. I don't want my baby to have a father like you. I don't want a husband like you either, so when you get home tonight, you pack your things and get out!' He looked so shocked and nervous, and he kept calling, 'Verona! Wait! Please don't go. This is nothing.' But I stood my ground and told him to pack his things and leave. I told him I'd tell everyone about the times he had struck me."

"Verona, I didn't know. Did he leave that night?"

"Well, he tried to soothe me, saying he loved me and would never do it again and if he left that night, where would he go?"

Worrying about himself, thought Addie.

"I stood my ground though and told him to go with his new girlfriend. I told him that being with her probably had been home for a while anyway."

Verona stopped talking. Addie searched for words of comfort, but could only find, "I'm so sorry."

"There's more." Verona struggled to begin again, pausing as though she were reluctant to tell it. When she finally spoke, the words came swiftly. "I was so upset and he was screaming at me, yelling that he wouldn't leave. I knew he would become physical, and I felt so trapped that I went to the bathroom and started to slash my wrists."

"No!" cried a shocked Addie.

"Jim called the hospital," Verona continued, "and I stayed there overnight. My wounds weren't deep, so I was all right physically, but not mentally. They called in a psychiatrist and a counselor. They were kind, but as I talked about it and answered their questions, I became sick to my stomach and then…" Verona became silent.

"Can you go on?" asked Addie.

"Well, you probably won't believe this, but all of a sudden, I had this amazing thing happen. I wasn't there. I had an out of body experience where I was up in the corner of the room, looking down at myself, the counselor and the psychiatrist. And do you know what? I didn't want to come back." She broke into sobs, repeating, "I really didn't want to come back."

Addie put her arms around her, comforting her like a mother soothing her child. "I wish you had told me what you were going through," she said. "You shouldn't have been by yourself, but I'm so glad you're back. Verona, things will get better." Then she asked quietly, "Are you pregnant?"

"No."

"Will Jim come back to town?"

"No. He's in California and can't come back. I have a court order prohibiting it."

Addie hugged her tightly and said, "I'm so proud of you for not letting Jim control your decisions and your actions. You are defending your rights as a woman, and I thank God for people like you." Excitedly she added, "And why don't you come and teach at Miller? With the teacher shortage there are lots of vacancies, and I know there is an elementary one at Miller. That would be a good spot for you. You could get a fresh start and maybe even take some classes at the university. I would love to have you there. Please, Verona, give it some thought."

"I will," answered Verona. "I just wish I had listened to you. You were right about him being a number one loser."

The telephone rang, interrupting their conversation. It was Ben, who invited them to dinner. He had made a wild rice casserole that would be ready in fifteen minutes.

Verona and Addie walked past the school and Mrs. Hugelstad's home to Ben's house.

The yard, in beautiful greenery, was enhanced by rose bushes and geraniums.

To see Ben is like coming home, thought Addie as he opened the door. Seeing his engaging smile, his horn-rimmed glasses, and familiar tweed jacket made her realize how much she wanted him to stay in her life.

Giving her a giant hug, he said, "I've missed you."

"I've missed you, too, and I also miss Roseland, the town, the students, my church, and even the noisy trains at two o'clock in the morning."

Ben laughed, then became serious. "I wish you could stay and make more memories."

"I can't, but I'm hoping we can hold on to the ones we have, and add to them, even if they're not all made right here."

He answered by nodding his head affirmatively and smiling as the doorbell rang again. Responding, he welcomed colleagues of Addie's who were spending the summer in Roseland. Verona, who had stayed outside to inspect Ben's flowers, brought in delicate pink roses for the table.

Ben guided Addie to the table and announced, "The honored guest is seated, so everyone to your places, please."

"It is so good to be back here and see so many of you," said Addie.

The evening went swiftly as she connected with each guest and found a lot to catch up on, even though she had been gone only a month. To Addie it seemed much longer. Her thoughts clouded as she thought of having to leave so soon, but she knew that to stay was an impossibility.

After the last guest had left, Addie felt Ben's arms around her.

"I'm so glad you're here," he said softly.

"I am too, Ben."

His kiss was long and intense, but Addie did not want to pull away. Finally, Ben drew back and put his arms on her shoulders.

"I don't want to lose you, Addie," he said. "We'll have to make it work from a distance."

"Others have done it," she responded.

They walked slowly back to Verona's house.

"I hope you'll come to Whitford soon," she said, "and so does my father. He's waiting to meet you."

"I'll be there," he promised. Hugging her tightly, he added, "I'll be there soon."

Two weeks went by without any word from Ben, but on the third weekend, he called and said that he would arrive Saturday afternoon.

"I can't work with you on Saturday," Addie informed her father. "Ben is coming."

Her father was silent. Addie knew he was thinking about the religious difference. Finally he said, "I guess you know I don't approve, but I'll make him welcome because it's your life and your decision."

"You'll like him, Dad. You can't help but like him."

"Only if he makes you happy."

As she finished setting the table for the noon lunch, Addie's mind wandered back to her college romance with Eric, remembering how hard it had been for her father to find words to console her, how much he had suffered because one of life's stings had penetrated his little girl, and there was nothing he could do to help.

Ben's maiden voyage to Whitford was during the middle of July. The rose bushes and geraniums decorating the front part of the house were in full array of color, enhanced by the green lawn and well trimmed shrubs.

Addie and her mother were sitting in lawn chairs enjoying the afternoon sun when Ben arrived. Addie rose to welcome him and introduce him to her mother. Before she could initiate the introduction, her mother grasped Ben's hand, saying, "I'm so glad to see you again. I thought that you and Addie were so beautiful at the prom."

Without flinching, Ben said gently, "Yes, Mrs. Carlson, that was one of the nicest times I have ever spent." He smiled at Addie and winked. Addie's mother was ecstatic.

"You must stay for supper. Addie worked so hard preparing it. She made such delicious…such delicious… Oh, Addie, I can't remember. What did you make?"

"Chicken, potatoes and gravy, creamed peas, and for dessert, apple pie. Supper will be at six o'clock. Dad is quitting early tonight so he can meet Ben."

Her father joined them promptly on the hour. Watching them, Addie sensed that their communication on any graphic measurement would be very high. It didn't surprise her, as Ben's "people power" was always evident, and her father had his own measure of quiet charm.

As they enjoyed the last morsels of the apple pie, Addie impulsively tried her own communicative powers.

"Ben," she said, "Mass is at eight o'clock tonight. We'll have to leave at seven-thirty."

"We?" he inquired incredulously.

"Sure," she said, "and then, maybe you could go to the Lutheran church with me tomorrow."

He stared at her. "It's just not done," he said. "The Catholic doctrine doesn't—"

"Just to visit, Ben."

He thought before answering, "I guess that would be all right, but I would have to takeoff right after church in the morning. I'm sorry to have to leave so early, but I have to be in Phoenix tomorrow night."

Addie was disappointed. "What for?" she asked, clearing the table.

"I was waiting to tell you," he said as he helped her put the remaining dishes in the sink, "that you're talking to the national president of the Rotary International. I'm going through my indoctrination on Monday."

"Congratulations," she said, giving him a hug. "Wish I had been there to help you celebrate."

He reminded her that she had zonked out at the mayor's race, but anyway, she would be invited to the first international junket as his guest.

"I accept," she said, adding pompously, "with full faith in your leadership. Good decision—smart too."

"I think I've heard that line before, Ben. I believe it was right after you were elected mayor."

They both laughed, remembering how she had gunned the gas pedal at Roseland in response to his same words and how the sound had awakened Mrs. Hugelstad, who immediately turned on her lights.

Father O'Malley welcomed them warmly to the mass. As both he and Ben had ties to St. John's, they reminisced briefly after the service.

Coming home, Ben explained parts of the service.

"I'd like to go again to understand the ritual better," said Addie.

Ben took his arms off the steering wheel momentarily, feigning shock.

"What would Martin Luther think?" he gasped. "Our ritual will soon be in English and will be easier to understand."

At the Lutheran church on Sunday, everyone crowded around the Carlson pew, hoping to be introduced to Addie's new beau. Even old Mr. Johnson, who used to visit Addie at the store and was now ninety years old, came over to talk and investigate.

Ben had to leave soon after the service, so Addie whisked him out the back door to his car. Giving her a goodbye hug, he whispered, "See you soon."

He got into his new Thunderbird, jokingly gunned the gas pedal in tribute to Mrs. Hugelstad, and drove away from Whitford and Addie.

Tending to her mother's needs and cooking for her family and the hired man made Addie's time at home pass quickly. The good news of the summer came in Verona's letter, saying she had signed a contract to teach fifth grade at Miller and had found an apartment only two blocks from the school. At the other end of the spectrum was frustration in watching her mother's decline in rational thought.

"Uncle Jeff was here," her mother would squeal. "I haven't seen him for such a long time."

"Mama, he's been dead for twenty years," Addie said quietly. Soon, however, she went along with her mother's imaginative reunions because, as her father said, "She's happier that way. I would rather see her smile than go into depression."

Just then her mother joined her, planting a kiss on Addie's cheek. "I've got to get the garden weeded before Mama comes," she said happily. "Addie, don't frown so. Come and help me now."

Addie smiled and joined her.

After Addie signed her contract at Miller, Superintendent Kelly asked her whether she had looked for a room or an apartment.

"I haven't decided whether I'll live here or at Whitford," she said.

The superintendent tapped his pencil on his desk, peered over his glasses and said, "I don't think you have a choice, Miss Carlson. Our school district policy mandates that teachers must live in the town in which they teach. You are paid by our taxes and we feel that the money you spend should return here."

Addie's face was flushed, but she spoke quietly, "I believe that state taxes also pay a share of my salary. I moved here in order to be near my family to help with medical problems. Whether I live here or in Whitford, I'll be spending many evenings with my folks, and I'll be buying groceries there as well as here. You know, Mr. Kelly, I know many people who commute from Whitford, including people who work in the court house. Certainly, they must be paid by tax money too."

Mr. Kelly seemed uncomfortable. Addie knew that the combined position of music and English was difficult to fill, and he needed her.

"Miss Carlson, we want you to become a member of our community, not Whitford's. That's all I want to say." As she began to leave, he said, "I'm glad you are joining our staff. You will be a fine addition…and I think, you'll enjoy the English and music combination."

"I hope so," she responded.

Addie expected apartment hunting to be a laborious task but, fortunately, found a small, inexpensive apartment close to school that she liked immediately. Even though Mrs. Hendrickson and other landladies had been kind and helpful, she felt a glorious sense of freedom as she roamed the tiny rooms of her new place.

The year began well at Miller. English students seemed respectful and the elementary music students were delightful. They held nothing back. They sang with their whole beings and gave honest answers. She loved their analogies. She smiled as she thought of the child who explained that a music descant was an ant that walked across the desk and another who thought that the northern star in "Minnesota, Hail to Thee" referred to their local North Star Laundry! Their ready smiles and enthusiasm entranced Addie as she entered their classrooms with a smile, a light heart, and a pitch pipe. Her smile widened as she thought of the education she received from the kindergartners on the opening day of school.

"We'll have a game," Addie had told them. "Let's make a circle." Their only response was to look at each other.

"It will be fun," she had said. "Let's all make a circle." They did. Fifteen little index fingers drew circles in the air.

On the first of December Addie's mother, who was getting weaker and more confused, was transferred to the local rest home. She seemed happy there, but she stayed in bed most of the time. When Addie and her father arrived at the home on Christmas Eve, her mother was excited about having dinner. When her meal arrived, Thor and Addie groaned at the sight of sweet soup, a Norwegian delicacy made of prunes, raisins, and other sweet mixtures that most Norwegian families really liked. Thor's family favorite, however, was *lutefisk*, a fish that had a gelatinous texture. The fish was usually accompanied by *lefse*, a thin bread product made primarily of potatoes and flour, usually rolled up and spread with butter and sugar.

"I'm going to send the soup back and demand something else," said Addie, but she was interrupted by her mother's joyous chatter. "I'm so happy that we have our lutefisk together tonight," she said. "I asked the cook to bring you some, too. And some more lefse. It is so good."

The server came with two big bowls of sweet soup accompanied by small pieces of lefse. "Isn't it good lutefisk?" asked her mother.

"It's wonderful," answered Addie, laughing. The tension seemed to dissolve, and her father joined in the laughter. Her mother was unsure what was going on, but she was happy, so she laughed too. They exchanged Christmas hugs that were long and words that were loving. Both Addie and her father knew this would be their last

Christmas with her, but they didn't know it would be the last night they would see her, that they soon would be called back to her room again.

As Addie entered the room that evening, her mother sat up, held up her arms weakly, and said, "I'm so glad you and your father are here—so glad."

"You must rest, Mom," cautioned Addie as she smoothed her sheets and tried to help her sit back.

Ignoring Addie's plea, she sat up again and motioned Thor to come closer.

"The Lord has given me clarity, perhaps only for the last minutes of my life," she said, "and I want to use it well."

Thor embraced his wife and nodded in agreement. Looking up at him, she said, "We had a good life, Thor."

"Yes, we did," he answered. As he clasped her hand in his, he said, "We were blessed with a wonderful daughter, too."

"Addie," said her mother, "come sit by me." Addie sat on the bed and held her mother's hand as she listened to her say, "Your father and I are so proud of you. You are using your gifts to help young people, and I don't know if there is a higher calling. I wanted to be a teacher once, too."

"I didn't know, Mom."

"But then I fell in love with your father, and at that time, you couldn't have both a husband and a teaching career. But I'm so happy you'll be able to have both."

Noticing she was tired, Thor suggested they pray the Lord's Prayer together and sing Marie's favorite song.

"Jesus Loves Me," said Marie happily.

They embraced one another and held hands as they sang the first verse and chorus. "Again," said Marie weakly. "Do it again,"

They repeated it again and again, then hummed the tune until Thor squeezed Addie's hand and said, "It's over."

Addie burst into tears and knelt by her mother's side. She looked up at her father and whispered, "I can't let her go, Dad. I just can't let her go."

Gently, Thor helped her rise and with his arm around her, they left the hospital.

The funeral was on December 27. Estelle was the soloist and relatives were pallbearers.

A phone call from Ben confirmed his plans to be at the funeral. Estelle would pick him up in Minneapolis, and he could drive back to Roseland with her after the service.

Addie greeted him with a warm hug, feeling comfort as she nestled momentarily against his tweed coat.

"I'm so glad you're here," she said.

Thor, too, seemed comforted by Ben's presence.

As Addie looked at all the beautiful flowers—many of them from relatives—she thought of the church split that had divided her cousins and uncles and aunts. She didn't remember the reason for the split and wondered if they did.

Her uncles and aunts were getting old, but Uncle Benjamin, who had once been over seven feet tall, still had to lean forward to get in the door. Aunt Ginger, the lunch connoisseur, was still curious about what would be served. Some of Addie's cousins had families she had scarcely met, but for today, they were all united in paying respects to a woman they loved regardless of church affiliation.

The sermon was short. As the burial would be in the spring, everyone met in the basement to express condolences and have a light lunch of sandwiches and cake.

Elsie Ross, her mother's cousin, was the first in line to express her sympathy.

"I loved Marie so much," she said, hugging Addie. "From the time I was eight years old, I wanted to be just like her. I wish I had come sooner, when she was alive."

"I know," comforted Addie, "but she really left us a long time ago, Elsie. You saw her at her best two years ago. I'm happy that you saw her when she was still the Marie you knew."

After a muffled sob, Elsie moved on, making room for other relatives, some of whom were younger ones who had gone to work in Minneapolis and were still home for Christmas vacation. Addie was happy to see them come.

The tempo of the conversations increased as people joined relatives and friends they hadn't seen for a long time. As the smell of Hills Brothers coffee permeated the small church, the laughter and spirited conversations seemed to mask, for the moment, the sadness of the occasion.

But soon the day was over. Estelle and Ben left late in the afternoon, leaving Addie and her father alone with their grief.

The days after Christmas were difficult ones for both Addie and her father. Addie took frequent trips back to Whitford during the week as well as weekends. Her father would sometimes surprise her with a dinner he had prepared, but often, they would eat at the local restaurant. Addie worried about her dad, but he assured her that like Thor, the mighty God of War, he was strong and would survive.

The weather had been uncharacteristically beautiful during March. As she drove to Whitford to enjoy spring break, the day was no exception. Her first night home gave her a feeling of contentment. To relax this fully is so wonderful, she thought as she felt herself drifting off into slumber.

She was awakened sharply by a rustling noise at her window, then heard a voice calling, "Ms. Carlson! It's Zane!"

Addie jumped out of bed, grabbed a robe, and ran to the front door, her mind racing as quickly as her steps. What is Zane doing here? How did he get here? What has happened to him?

"Over here, Zane," she said as she opened the door. Her voice changed to a whisper as she took his arm.

"My father is asleep, so I can't turn on the lights. I'll guide you to the study where we can talk."

When she turned on the lights of the study, she was surprised to see how thin he had become. Silently he gazed at the floor, seeming not to meet her eyes, but finally the words came in a torrent.

"I'm sorry, Ms. Carlson, but I jist couldn't stay there another night. I felt bad 'bout breakin' out 'cuz Sheriff Barton was really pretty good to me, but I couldn't stand jail no longer. I've been there almost two years for nothin'. I didn't do nothin', Ms. Carlson. If this is the democracy you told me about, I don't want it. It ain't fair."

Addie was unprepared for Zane's tears trickling down his cheeks. *He looks so young, so vulnerable, so tired and frightened*, she thought.

"How did you get out, Zane?" asked Addie, sitting down in an arm chair facing Zane.

He said that a friend helped him get out and made connections for a ride to the train, but he would not tell where the money came from. He said that he didn't steal—that it was legal.

Addie wondered if Miss Maribelle's sugar bowl of money saved through the years had anything to do with Zane's escape. She also pondered how he got out. She knew Sheriff Barton often brought in young deputies to work relief shifts. Could one of them have been careless in locking Zane's cell? Could someone have left it open intentionally? She knew they had a special feeling for this young man caught in the wrong place at the wrong time, and they knew he was beginning to give in to his despair.

"One more question, Zane," said Addie, "and then I'll let you rest. How did you find my house?"

"Well, in your last letter, you said you were going to spend your spring vacation at Whitford. When you first came to Alabama, you showed me many pictures of your parents' house and gave me instructions how to find it in case I ever needed you, so I wrote it down. You told me it was only a mile from town, and you walked that road a lot. The house and the road were easy to find, but I had to walk fast because it was getting dark.

"When I got to your house, I hid in the hedges until I saw a light go out in one of your rooms. I guessed it would come on in a bedroom and it did. I was really happy to hear your voice, though, because I could have gotten your father's bedroom."

"That's right," said Addie flatly as she tried to conquer her fatigue from a busy workweek. "Tell you what, Zane. We have sandwiches in the refrigerator. I'll bring you lunch and a glass of milk. Then I'll make up the couch and you can sleep here tonight."

When she returned from the kitchen, he was looking at family photographs on the wall.

The tired teenager turned as she entered.

"Try to sleep, Zane," Addie said as she put sheets on the couch. "We'll decide what to do tomorrow."

"All right, Ms. Carlson. Good night."

Addie shut the door to the study and tiptoed back to her room. Fatigue was replaced by "second wind" energy as questions raced through her mind. Should she call Sheriff Barton the first thing in the morning? Zane would think she was abandoning him. She needed help from someone who could respect and understand Zane's predicament. Finally she decided to call Hank and Ginny at Peoria. She knew Hank's law office didn't open until nine o'clock, but hopefully, she would catch him at home before he left for work.

During the night, a surprised Thor met Zane on the way to the bathroom. Quickly finding Addie, he excitedly asked, "Why didn't you let me know? Who is he? What is he doing here?" Pacing the hallway, he reminded her that he had never known a black man. "Now, I find him in my bathroom in the middle of the night. How do you expect me to act?"

Addie grasped his hand. "I'm so sorry, Dad, so sorry. Everything happened so fast, and I slept longer than I had planned."

Addie recounted the night's events.

"What are you going to do, Addie?" asked her father, nervously pacing. "You can get in trouble for shielding him. You've got to send him back."

"Don't worry, Dad, I'm calling Hank and Ginny right now. I need Hank's legal advice. It's eight o'clock now, and I'm hoping to catch him before he leaves for the office."

Ginny's high-pitched, excited voice responded to Addie's call.

"Addie," Ginny squealed, "I haven't heard from you for so long. It's wonderful to hear your voice again. I was going to call you, but I've only been home from the hospital a couple days. We have another child, an adorably sweet little girl. And get this, we named her Addie."

"Really?"

"After Hank's aunt," said Ginny, who paused a moment, then started to giggle. "No, Addie," she said, "I was kidding. We don't even know another Addie. Hank and I decided long ago that if we ever had a daughter, she would be named after you. I want her to be just like you, so you'll have to come out and supervise. Oh, here's Hank. He wants to say hello."

After congratulating Hank on the birth of his daughter, Addie told him about Zane's dilemma. Hank hesitated before answering. "I don't know a lawyer in that vicinity, but I'm on my way to the office now. I'll look through my national directory to find one from that area who specializes in racial situations, but I would advise you to get Zane on a flight to Montgomery today. If I find a lawyer who I think would be suitable, I'll ask him to meet Zane at the Montgomery airport, which is forty miles from Selma, and deliver him to the Selma sheriff. If I don't find one, we'll have to call the sheriff directly. I'll get on this right away and I'll call you back this morning."

True to his word, Hank called back at eleven-thirty. "Good news," he said. "I found a lawyer who is held in high regard by the National Bar Association. He has, in fact, served as vice president of the group. His name is Jared Magnum, and he'll meet Zane's plane. There's a Northwest flight leaving from Minneapolis in two hours and tickets are available. Can you make it?"

"Yes, it's only forty miles from here."

Reviewing the plans, Hank again cautioned her to be sure to get him on Flight 46 to Montgomery where Mr. Magnum would hold up a sign with the name and address of the Magnum Law Office. She should tell Zane to look for it.

The good news Hank offered was that Mr. Magnum was really interested in Zane's case, so every effort should be made to get to Montgomery as soon as possible.

Addie informed Zane of the arrangement. Telling both Zane and her father to hurry, she grabbed her purse and went to the garage to start her car. Shortly they were driving down a side street, relieved that it was a quiet day with few people around.

Soon, Zane was in the sky, and Addie and her father were back home. That evening, Hank called, telling them that Mr. Magnum had accomplished the mission and was already checking the background of Zane's case.

"How is Zane?" asked Addie.

"Fine, I guess," answered Hank. "Sheriff Barton seemed greatly relieved to get him back, but he didn't say much. He just said that they took him to his cell and they would talk the next morning."

"Do you think this has hurt his case a lot, Hank?"

"Couldn't help but hurt it some. A breakout is serious. But don't worry so much. Get some sleep, and try to forget this ordeal."

With Hank's compassionate words, she tried to relax and turn her focus to school, but it didn't work. She kept hearing Zane's voice crying "I didn't do nothin', Ms. Carlson, and I've been in this stinkin' jail for almost two years."

Nature's process of "greening up" in spring time served to raise Addie's spirits from the despondency she had experienced with her mother's death. As the crop yield from the previous year had been slight and farmers in the area were in financial trouble, she promised her father she would help him with the farm work during summer vacation. She loved driving the Allis Chalmers tractor that she named Goliath because of its size. She would have enjoyed the power of the combine too, but her father preferred to have her drive the truck. Despite rather negative feelings about weeding vegetables, she decided that she would plant potatoes, carrots, tomatoes, green beans, squash, and even watermelon. It would be a busy summer on the farm, relieved only by her visit to the National Education Association meeting in Atlantic City during the first week in July. As incoming president of the local teachers' association, she wanted to experience the national organization firsthand. She had served on the negotiations committee during the previous year and fought hard against salary discrepancies. She vividly remembered her second year in Roseland, before salary schedules were in effect. She had received a $50 raise from the Superintendent Almighty, while the teacher in the next room was given $150.

"Why? Am I not doing my job?" she had asked.

"Oh yes," the superintendent had gushed, "but we hired you at a greater salary than we gave others when they started here."

She remembered biting her lip and making a quick exit.

In Roseland, she had criticized the policy of giving $150 to all married male teachers as a benefit for being the head of the household. This benefit was not extended to women, but Addie thought the policy should be dropped completely. She felt that marital status should have no bearing on teacher salaries or benefits. Also, she questioned why a husband and wife team could not teach in the same school.

"Fuddy-duddy, unfair rules," complained Addie. "I'm amazed they finally let married women teach." She remembered that when she was a child, the school board found out that Addie's beloved third grade teacher, Miss Pringle, had been secretly married. In a week, Miss Pringle was gone, and Addie did not like her replacement. She cried herself to sleep many nights that year, and her grades took a nosedive. Her mother and father were heartsick, but they could not overrule the school's decision.

May was countdown time for both teachers and students. Final tests, themes, and speeches had to be graded. Declamation students had been successful in the regional contest, so they must now keep working for the state meet in May. Some of the noon hours involved rehearsals for the elementary students' concerts as well as work with speech contestants. It was check-in and check-out time for written work and books. It was a mental check-out month for students. Their attention wavered and the outdoors beckoned.

Then it was over.

The senior class walked down the aisle. Addie felt a lump in her throat as she realized suddenly she would not see these students ever again in the classroom situation, and some, she may never see again. Feeling like a mother checking the list as her children went off to college, she wondered if they understood what she meant about being careful and responsible, and did they realize how hard they would have to study in college to make it. Finally, she wondered if they knew how much she cared about them.

Then her worries gave way to pride as she watched them march to the strains of "Pomp and Circumstance." As they approached the platform to receive their diplomas, she wondered if any would remember the story of the sparrow.

The month of June was busy for Addie. Gardening, cooking, driving tractor and acting as an errand girl for her father took most of her time, but she loved the work and the sense of accomplishment it gave her.

After watering her flowers on a beautiful June morning, she looked up to see her father coming from the mailbox, excitedly waving a letter in his hand and calling, "It's from Nigeria, Addie."

Running to meet him, she eagerly took the letter and opened it.

"I answered an advertisement in a teachers' magazine to go to Nigeria for six weeks beginning a year from next July," she said. "My job would be to teach in one of the Christian schools and to assess the student tests that are given each year by the West African Examination Council."

Her father's expression was worried.

"It's just an application form, Dad, but if I am accepted, I'll be just fine," comforted Addie. "I'm really interested in the project, and I'd like to see Africa."

Her father struggled a little as he responded, "Sure, Addie. It will be all right. I think you should take the opportunity if it comes."

As she walked back to the house with her father, she noticed that his gait was not as steady as usual.

"It's the weather," he said. "The dampness cuts to the bones, you know."

The Atlantic City convention brought teachers from every state in the union. They argued issues, spoke from experience, and worked for change. Addie was happy that many of the issues for which she battled were already in resolution form to advocate change. Early morning state delegation meetings were held before representatives presented new resolutions to the national forum. Impressive speeches by colleagues made Addie proud to be a teacher. She was unprepared, however, for the statements by a representative of the Health, Education and Welfare Department.

"My dear friends!" he boomed. "This is a precarious time for educators and for the future of education. You can work for change, but you must realize that the public's confidence in education is erased when an association strikes. I know some of you are contemplating this action, but I feel that I must warn you that a strike will provide the death-knell for public support. Improvement of public education will suffer a severe setback. I implore you. Do not strike!"

"No one wants to strike," said Addie to another delegate. "We know that it would take time to build trust again, but what is he saying? Just let things go along as they are? Times are changing and he wants us to go on as though we still lived when teachers had to build their own fires and do their own janitorial work."

"I'm with you, Addie," answered the delegate, "but if you decide you need to strike, can't you imagine the job of convincing an entire local teachers' association to go along with you? Think of the women who are teaching to supply a second income for their families and who may be influenced or even compelled by their husbands to vote against a strike. Also, consider the two-year teachers who can't get jobs very easily because more schools are demanding four years of college education. Unity will be hard to achieve. Strike is an ugly word."

"I know it's an ugly word," Addie answered, "but sometimes it takes conflict to bring change, whether it be a strike or just standing up and speaking against a majority view."

"You're right, Addie, and if another association feels it's necessary for them to strike to further their cause, really our cause too, then we need to stand behind them."

"Agreed," said Addie as they parted.

Chapter 7

TRIAL

When Addie arrived home from the convention, her father was eating his lunch. "There's some mail," he said. "A letter from that Magnum lawyer came."

"Really?" asked Addie. "I wonder what he wants."

"Probably a subpoena," replied her father, jokingly.

Addie laughed until she opened it and realized her father was right.

"That's what it is. Zane's case is set for August 28, and I'm being called as a witness for him. Mr. Magnum says that he's the lawyer for the defense. I'm so glad that he's taking Zane's case. I'll call Hank and tell him."

Hank had already heard the news and had been in contact with Magnum.

"He's a good lawyer," said Hank. "Being a black man himself, he understands what Zane is up against. For credentials, how does *magna cum laude* from Georgetown University grab you?"

"Very good. I'll be looking forward to meeting him in Montgomery."

The summer went fast. Addie spent a lot of time in her garden and actually found herself enjoying it. She even canned some of the vegetables and a lot of rhubarb sauce, her father's favorite. The crops looked good, and by the middle of August, they were done harvesting.

Addie boarded a plane for Montgomery on August 27. She took a cab to a hotel near the courthouse and tried to relax, but couldn't. So much depended on this trial. She wondered how Zane was coping. She wondered about the makeup of the jury and the reputation of the judge.

Unable to rest, she went to the window and looked out at the lights of Montgomery. It was ten thirty at night, and the city hummed with the usual noise of cars, music, voices, and sirens.

The Baptist Church on the corner reminded her of the one in Selma. She remembered their beautiful choir and their differences in performance as they accompanied their singing with rhythmical body movements and percussive sounds. She thought of the wonderful times she had shared with Miss Maribelle and her family before the accident.

Then her mind went to the airport in Minneapolis and to Ben. In her latest letter, Estelle wrote that Ben had been dating Sue Callahan, the teacher who had replaced Addie. "They work a lot together on committees at church," she wrote. "I don't think it's serious because he always asks if I have heard from you and if you are seeing anyone."

The letter upset her much more than she thought it would. Ben had come to Whitford occasionally, but she had not seen him since the middle of July, and his letters seemed to be slow in coming. She wanted to be happy for Ben if he found happiness with someone else, but in all truth, she knew it would be difficult for her to accept the news. Knowing he would remember their pact and honor it, she tried not to worry, but she did.

In spite of Estelle's words of comfort, Addie felt she needed to hear from Ben. *After all*, she thought, *he's dating someone else, and I need to know if it's serious or not*. She also thought she needed to know because she felt the life she wanted, especially one with Ben, was moving out of her grasp. Inwardly, she moaned that she could not handle another roadblock.

In the same letter, Estelle announced she would be leaving Roseland at the end of the coming school year.

"I'll be teaching voice at the McPhail School of Music in St. Paul," she wrote, "and, hopefully, conducting some community choirs, as well as the choir at my church. I'm happy for this opportunity, not only professional ones but also because I met an interesting man at Christmastime. He works for a new food company in Minneapolis that actually encourages blacks to advance in the company."

She closed her letter with a philosophical glimmer that Addie had grown to expect from her.

"We can't change the world," she wrote, "but maybe we can help lift it up a notch." Addie shut the windows and drew the drapes to shut out the noises of the street. The *Wizard of Oz* was on TV, and as she looked at the lion, the tin man, and the scarecrow, she empathized with them, knowing that like the scarecrow she must use her brain, like the lion she must have courage, and like the tin man she must have a good heart. She prayed for strength and courage, for tomorrow would be a difficult day.

The flowers were still in full bloom, and their scent filled the air as Addie left for the court house the next morning. She breathed deeply and gazed at the gorgeous colors. It seemed such a pity, she thought, to leave the beauty and fragrance of the outdoors to enter the dark legal corridors and inhale the air of a building that had been closed all weekend.

As she reached the top of the last flight of stairs, she saw Zane talking to a well-dressed black man who she assumed was Jared Magnum. He was of average height and stocky build, with wavy grey hair and rimless glasses.

Seeing Zane dressed in prison clothes was difficult, but he seemed happy to see her, and he proudly introduced Mr. Magnum.

"I've heard a lot about you, Miss Carlson, both from Zane and from Hank Emmens," said Magnum. "You'll be a great help in establishing his character."

"I'll do my best," Addie said, smiling.

At nine o'clock, the first witness for the prosecution was called. Addie was annoyed to see Nate Pomeroy step up. "He was in my class," whispered Addie to Mr. Magnum. "I thought he was a friend of Zane's."

"Could be, but he is vulnerable. The prosecution may have reached him with a lot of smooth talk and, maybe, an appealing reward like a trip to Selma, a night in a hotel and great meals."

Nate took the stand and was sworn in. When he saw Addie, he looked away, seeming not to recognize her.

"Nate," said the prosecutor, "how do you know Zane Smith?"

"Went to school with him."

"Is he a friend?"

"Well…maybe."

"Why are you hesitant, Nate?"

"He's rough, always starting fights."

"Did he ever hit you?"

"Yup," said Nate, looking down. "He even said he'd kill me the next time."

Addie whispered to Magnum, "Zane said that they did a lot of 'roughhousing' in school, but it was always in fun. If he said he'd kill him the next time, he probably meant that he would win the next 'roughhouse' game."

As the prosecution finished, Magnum stood to cross examine Nate. "Nate," he said softly, "what did you do last night?"

"Objection. Irrelevant."

"Your Honor, I can prove the relevance in the next few questions."

"Overruled. Witness may answer."

"What did you do last night?" repeated Magnum.

"I went to the movies with my friend, Jeremiah," he answered, pointing to a young man in the front row.

"Have you ever been to a movie in Selma before?"

"Just once."

"Did you stay in a hotel last night?"

"Yup."

"Which one?"

Nate said proudly, "The Admiral."

"That's a pretty fancy hotel, Nate. Have you ever stayed in a hotel before?"

"Nope."

"Did you enjoy it?"

The audience smiled as Nate vividly described the TV—the games—cokes, and even the beds that were pulled down from the wall.

Continuing his cross-examination, Magnum said, "Nate, you are under oath now, and I need the truth, so think carefully. When Zane gave you a black eye, was it accidental?"

"I don't think so. He punched me hard."

"Were you 'roughhousing' at the time?"

"Well, yes."

"When he said, 'I'll kill you next time,' couldn't he have meant that he would win the game again? Isn't that possible?"

"I-I-I don't know."

"Have you ever said, 'I'll kill you next time' when you wanted to let someone know you planned to win the next game?"

"Well, I guess…"

Looking at the prosecutor's stern countenance, Nate quickly said, "I don't remember."

"That's all," said Magnum. "You can step down now."

Another of Addie's students, Jeremiah Jones, took the stand. His testimony was almost identical to Nate's until the prosecutor switched his focus.

"Jeremiah," he asked, "did Zane Smith ever talk about a gun?"

"Yeah," answered Jeremiah.

"Did you and your friends ever see it?"

"No. Zane never showed it to us, but he said he had one."

"Did he say he knew how to use it?"

"Sure. He said he had to know how to in order to protect his grandmama. He lived with her."

"Thank you, Jeremiah," said the prosecutor.

Magnum did not cross-examine, so Jeremiah stepped down. For just a moment, his eyes met Addie's as he walked past her, but he averted his gaze and hurried to his seat.

"Don't these kids know what they're doing?" asked Addie.

"I don't think they understand the impact," answered Magnum.

The next witness was Jordan Pollard, a young white male who at the time of the shooting on May 8 at 6:30 p.m., had been sitting in his car, waiting for his wife to come out of the Bartel Grocery Store. He testified that he heard a shot and saw Miss Hyde's boyfriend, who had been standing by her car parked two rows in front of him, fall to the ground. He ran to help, but Miss Hyde was already kneeling down by her boyfriend, who she said had died instantly. Mr. Pollard said he ran back to the store to call the police, and when he returned, Miss Hyde said she had seen a black man running to his car like the devil was after him.

Mr. Pollard stepped down, and Loretta Hyde, whose boyfriend, Tom Nicolet, had been killed, was the last witness for the prosecution. She was a curvaceous brunette with brown hair and blue eyes who wore a pretty red figured dress, accented with gold bracelets and earrings. After she took the oath, the prosecution approached her and asked where she had been when the shooting occurred. She stated that she was coming out of Bartel's Grocery Store to join her boyfriend, Tom Nicolet, who was standing by her car. She heard a shot and saw Tom fall. She rushed to his side, but he had died instantly. Mr. Pollard came to help, but when Miss Hyde told him that Tom had died, he ran back to the store to call the police. When he returned, Miss Hyde said she had seen a black man running to his car.

"How far away from the suspect were you when you saw him running to his car?" asked the prosecution.

"Only about twelve feet, and I could see him just fine. I recognized him easily in the lineup the next morning."

The prosecutor smiled and thanked her.

Mr. Magnum approached the witness. "Miss Hyde," he said, "Did the man you saw running to his car have a gun?"

"I didn't see one on him, but he could have had one in his pocket. He wore a long shirt that could have covered it."

"But isn't it possible that someone else could have crowded between the cars, and shot Mr. Nicollet and left without anyone seeing him?"

"Objection!" stormed the prosecutor. "The defense is calling for speculation by the witness."

"Sustained," said the judge.

As Mr. Magnum approached her, he took a letter from his pocket. "To the Judge," he said, "I have here a letter from her doctor stating that the vision in her left eye has suffered due to an accident. Is that correct, Miss Hyde?"

"I suppose, but I can see just fine."

"Your Honor," said Mr. Magnum, "because of the medical issue involved, I would like to ask the Court's permission to challenge Miss Hyde's vision."

The judge peered over his glasses at Magnum. He thought a moment, then said, "Because of the medical issue involved, I think we can allow it."

A "Perry Mason" drama unfolded as four men walked to the right of the judge's bench.

Miss Hyde stood near the back of the courtroom, approximately twelve feet away.

"Now, Miss Hyde," he said, "I want you to look at these four men carefully and when you are ready, tell me if the man who killed your boyfriend is up there, and if so, which one is he?"

Her gaze went from left to right, and her questioning eyes moved slowly from one to another. She carefully studied the features of each man and finally she pointed to the man farthest to the right. Confidently, she said, "This is the man."

As if on cue, the side door to the courtroom opened, and Zane, joined the lineup.

The judge said, "Let the records show that Zane Smith was not the person identified by Miss Hyde."

Loretta Hyde stepped down, still shaking her head, visibly upset.

To Addie the first witnesses for the defense were only mildly effective. The gardener Zane had worked for briefly described him as a good worker, while Mr. Long, the principal of the high school, portrayed Zane as an average student who got along well with his classmates. He said they all liked to "roughhouse," but he didn't see that any of them had a propensity for violence, even though he felt that prevailing racial unrest could certainly stimulate such behavior.

Addie's interest piqued when Darren Holbrook, a younger student, approached the stand. He was small of stature, wore thick glasses, and walked with a limp. He described Zane as a friend at school who would sometimes walk home with him to protect him from some other kids.

When asked about the gun, Darren said he never did see one, but Zane told him it had been stolen a month before school was out. And Zane thought some boys in his class had taken it.

Knowing she was next, Addie felt apprehensive. *I need to calm down*, she thought. *I won't be any use to Zane if I become unglued.*

She looked at the pictures on the front wall. One was of a lion that had a Latin inscription beneath the picture. Again she thought of the cowardly lion in the *Wizard of Oz* who always made her smile. Feeling more relaxed, she took the stand. After she identified herself and took the oath, Mr. Magnum asked her where she had met Zane. Addie answered that she had met him in jail in June 1966, where she was a teacher working with TICEP and he was a student. She described him as a hard worker, especially on themes. He loved John F. Kennedy and believed strongly in democracy, but he was unable to understand why he had to stay in jail for a crime he didn't commit."

"Objection," call the prosecutor.

"Sustained," said the judge.

"How would you describe Zane's personality, Miss Carlson?" continued Magnum.

"He is friendly and outgoing. I see Zane as an honest young man who has dealt with a difficult life in an admirable way. He never knew his parents. He was raised by his grandmother. When she became ill, he cared for her until she entered a nursing home where she died soon after."

"What do you think happened to his gun?" queried Magnum.

"If Zane said it was stolen, then I'm sure it was," answered Addie. "People had every opportunity to steal it after his grandmother moved to the home. Zane, admittedly, did not always lock his doors, and many youngsters knew about the gun."

"Miss Carlson, do you believe Zane had enough rage in him to shoot a helpless man at random?"

"No, I don't. I know him to be a gentle person. He is not a violent young man."

"Thank you, Miss Carlson," said Magnum.

Addie's apprehension heightened as the prosecutor approached.

"Miss Carlson," he said, "you describe Zane, in your own words, as a proponent of democracy and, of course, freedom. As his teacher, did you help him understand that democracy also means responsibility and adherence to the laws of this country? He broke the law by breaking out of jail and running to find you. How do you explain that?"

"He was young and terrified. For over two years, he had longed for freedom, but he was running out of hope for a trial that might give it to him."

The prosecutor leaned forward, assuming what to Addie was a deferential pose.

"Miss Carlson," he said, "it is one thing to cry for freedom and democracy when you're behind bars, but to practice it on the outside is a different matter. Didn't you realize he was bidding for your sympathy and your help to conceal the fact that he is a cold-blooded murderer?"

Magnum objected and it was sustained.

"Your Honor, could I answer the prosecution's question?" asked Addie.

"Will the defense withdraw its objection?" asked the judge.

"Yes," responded Magnum, "if the witness wants to answer the question, we will withdraw the objection."

Firmly, Addie said, "No, Zane did not ask me for any help because of any guilt. He asked for help because, as a teacher, I had told him that if mistakes are made in a democracy, they can be corrected. He felt he was falsely identified in the lineup, and he wanted it rectified."

"Miss Carlson," said the prosecutor in his well-modulated tones, "I submit that you, as a teacher, have done irreparable harm to your profession by aiding and shielding a prisoner accused of a heinous crime."

Magnum was on his feet. "Miss Carlson is not on trial here," he said vigorously. "I request that the remarks by the prosecutor be stricken from the records."

The request was granted. The prosecutor had finished his questioning.

Magnum decided that Zane would be strong in his own defense, so he called him forward to testify. He knew it was a risky venture, but hopefully one that would work with the jury. Zane looked nervous. Magnum smiled at him, trying to calm the fidgety young man whose long legs could not seem to find a stationary position.

"Zane," said Mr. Magnum. "Tell us what you were doing in Selma on the evening of May29, 1966."

Zane answered, "I went to an early movie. I went alone because all of my friends had already seen it."

When asked the name of the movie, he looked uncomfortable but said, "*That Darn Cat.*"

There was a slight twitter in the audience, but Magnum continued quickly. "What happened after the movie, Zane?"

He described walking to the parking lot about two blocks away, where he had parked his car. He heard a shot, and it scared him, so he started to run, then ducked down behind a nearby car in case another shot came. When it didn't come, he got up and ran to his own car.

He said the police soon came, dragged him out of the car, and took him to jail. They said a white man had been killed and his girlfriend said she saw a black man trying to get away. They told him he would be in a lineup in the morning.

"How many were in the lineup?" asked Mr. Magnum.

"I think it was five," answered Zane. "Miss Hyde said I was the shooter, and they took me to jail."

"Did you kill Mr. Nicollet, Zane?"

Zane's voice boomed, "No! I don't even know who the man was." His voice quieted as he said, "I jist wanted to see a movie."

"One more question, Zane. When was your grandmother's gun stolen?"

"Before school was over. A little over a month before."

"Thank you, Zane. No more questions."

It was the prosecutor's turn.

Addie was proud of Zane as he responded to the prosecutor's attempts to throw him off track. He stuck to his story and rebutted the lawyer's attempts to create a different scenario.

Zane admitted he was wrong in breaking out of jail, and he listened quietly as the prosecutor told him that running away is the action of a guilty man who wants to "fly the coop" and not pay for the terrible crime he has committed.

"Mr. Smith," the prosecutor concluded, "the defense has painted you as a poor, innocent victim who was in the wrong place at the wrong time. But isn't that a fairy tale? Isn't the truth that you went to Selma for a movie, and your gun was concealed under your shirt, and after the movie, you went into one of your violent rages. It was a rage like the ones you exhibited on the school grounds. Then you shot Mr. Nicolet at random. Isn't that correct, Mr. Smith?"

"No, no," said Zane shaking his head.

"I submit that your gun was not stolen, that you took it along to Selma for a purpose, and that the only one who was in the wrong place at the wrong time was Mr. Nicolet. Isn't that right?" asked the prosecutor.

"Objection," said Magnum. "He is harassing the defendant."

"Sustained," said the judge.

The prosecution quickly ended its interrogation of Zane, who stepped down from the stand.

It was time for summations by the attorneys. The prosecutor's summation was first.

"Ladies and gentlemen," he said, "our evidence has proved that Mr. Smith has a long record of violence dating back to schoolyard, hitting and threatening. That violence erupted again at Selma, where he killed Mr. Nicollet at random and sped to his car to try to get away and escape the consequences of his act. Now, we realize that identification can sometimes be flawed, and we admit that Miss Hyde made an error of recognition in the lineup. However, you must remember that Mr. Pollard, who was also at the scene, did not see another suspect either. Mr. Smith was the only one around, and he fled after the murder because he was guilty.

"The defense is painting their client as a victim. 'He just happened to be running to his car at the time Mr. Nicollet was shot,' they are saying. 'His gun just happened to be stolen before he went to Selma.' This is not a true picture, ladies and gentlemen. When you look back at Mr. Smith's record of playground violence and the rage that caused him to attack his friends, you must agree with the prosecution that Zane Smith knew what he was going to do in Selma. And he did it! He shot a poor, unsuspecting man who was waiting for his girlfriend. Consequently, he not only took a man's life, but he also ruined Miss Hyde's hopes for a future with the man she loved.

Then he said in conclusion, "Ladies and gentlemen, Mr. Smith is a young man whose predilection for violence makes him a danger to society. He will continue to shoot at random and kill innocent people. Therefore, you must bring back a verdict of guilty."

Then it was Magnum's turn. He faced the jury. "Ladies and gentlemen," he began firmly. "You have sat patiently through an exercise in judicial history that never should have been. A man has been on trial because he ran to his car at the wrong time. He ran because he was scared, just as you would have been if you heard a shot and were a young black man in Selma at this time of unrest. He had a right to be scared.

"Now, the prosecution has made a playground game into something sinister. It has taken the 'I'll kill you next time' game challenge and put it into the context of a murder threat. It is a gimmick, ladies and gentlemen, a gimmick employed by the prosecution because they have no credible motive or evidence." Magnum's voice became quieter. "Mr. Smith is not a violent man, but he is getting impatient for freedom that he feels is rightfully his. Miss Hyde falsely identified him in the lineup, and because of that, he has sat in jail for over two years, waiting for a trial that he believes will set him free because he is innocent."

Magnum paused and moved closer to the jury. "When you leave your jury duty," he said slowly and deliberately, "this experience will be behind you, but Mr. Smith will have to live with your verdict for the rest of his life. You cannot, in good conscience, convict him on the evidence offered by the prosecution. The holes are too large, the truth is not there. Zane Smith is innocent of any wrongdoing. When you are deliberating, remember that you are sealing the fate of a young man who has already been unfairly treated, and that you, the jury, are the only ones who can end this fiasco by returning a verdict of 'not guilty.'"

The jury left the room in silence.

Zane and Mr. Magnum were busy conferring when Addie stopped to congratulate Zane on his testimony and Mr. Magnum on his legal expertise.

"What do you think Zane's chances for acquittal are?" asked Addie.

"I really don't know. I'm hoping the Martin Luther King marches may exert some influence, but I can't predict victory. You can never foresee the results of a trial, especially when it involves race."

Mr. Magnum took a white handkerchief from his pocket and mopped the perspiration from his brow. Zane also showed discomfort from the heat.

"I wish they'd get the fans working. It's unbelievably warm in here," said Mr. Magnum, finally removing his jacket. "I think we should all leave. Miss Carlson, why don't you go out and get some air? Zane and I will look for another cooler place."

Addie was happy to go outside and inhale the smell of the green grass and flowers she had admired just two hours earlier before entering the court room. She took deep breaths, not seeming to get enough of nature's delicate fragrances, but not even her enjoyment of such beauty could keep her thoughts from Zane and his ordeal. She prayed for justice.

Suddenly she heard children's voices. Turning, she was surprised to see Rebecca, Zelda, John, and the children coming down the court house steps.

"Surprise!" they called.

"It is a surprise," said Addie, laughing. "I didn't see you in court."

The twins, now four-years-old, seemed to remember Addie, and they held out their arms to her. As she sat on the courthouse steps, holding Lucy first, then Missy, she experienced again the contentment of feeling their faces against hers and their little arms around her neck. She hated to let them go.

"Where did you all sit?" she asked John.

"Rebecca and the twins stayed outside, but Zelda, Miss Maribelle, and I sat in the last three seats to the left in the back row."

"Miss Maribelle is here?" asked Addie in astonishment.

"Course I'm here!" called Miss Maribelle as she walked down the steps with the help of both the railing and her cane. "We missed you last summer, Addie."

"And I missed all of you." Addie answered.

They exchanged pleasantries and "catch-up" information, but even with conversations between good friends who hadn't seen each other for over two years, time seemed to lag. The light talk seemed superfluous to Addie in relation to the tense drama occurring upstairs in the courthouse. She brought greetings from Estelle and informed the group that between Roseland and Miller, proceeds from lounge treats and other ventures should approach $3,500 to be given to the library.

"Lord be praised!" said Miss Maribelle. "It makes me feel trembleacious."

Taking Miss Maribelle aside, Addie pressed a hundred dollar bill into her hand, saying, "Miss Maribelle, before I left, I wanted to contribute to your sugar bowl fund but I left so quickly I didn't have a chance. I need to do this, so please don't say no."

Miss Maribelle looked up at Addie after glancing at the denomination of the bill. She smiled as she accepted the currency, and to Addie's astonishment, she winked at her. Addie laughed, for now, she was sure that Miss Maribelle had sponsored Zane's trip to Whitford. Knowing Miss Maribelle, she wasn't surprised.

"Shouldn't the jury be back by now?" asked Zelda, looking at her watch. Both she and Zach looked worried. Addie shared their apprehension. She had heard that if a jury deliberated for a long time, there was more chance for a conviction. The last half hour had passed with little conversation. Addie hated the silence. It gave her an ominous feeling, but she reassured herself by thinking of the strength of Zane's defense. She waffled from feeling a deep faith in the jury system to fearing they would give unjustified credence to the prosecution's case.

Her waffling was interrupted by the bailiff. He called them back to the courtroom, stating that the jury was once again assembled. The foreman was already standing, ready to read the verdict to Zane and Mr. Magnum, who also stood for the reading. Addie's breath seemed to stop. Miss Maribelle's eyes were closed, and Addie was sure she was praying.

The silence was broken only by the faint sound of a bird chirping outside the courthouse window. The foreman cleared his throat and, with very slow pacing, began reading the verdict, a verdict that could save or destroy Zane's life. "We find the defendant, Zane Smith." He paused a moment before the strong clear words "Not guilty!" rang through the courtroom.

Zane's shoulders relaxed as he heard the verdict. He turned to Mr. Magnum and shook his hand, then Addie's. But there was no time to celebrate as shouts of dissatisfaction with the verdict came from both inside and outside of the building. People exited quickly, fearing violence.

Addie took a quick look at Miss Maribelle and her people, waved goodbye, and went quickly to her waiting cab. She did not relax until the plane was in the air on its way to Minneapolis.

Quickly, she penned a note to Ben, telling him about the trial and of her happiness with the outcome.

In conclusion, she wrote, "I have really missed you, Ben, and pray that distance will not prove too strong a barrier to our relationship." She closed her note as usual with "Hope to see you soon," but added, "we need to talk."

Chapter 8

TEACHER STRIKE

Addie began her second year at Miller with a strong commitment to serve a successful term as president of the Miller Teachers' Association. She became consumed with strike worries when the school board wanted to add two additional work days to the school calendar while offering only a 2 percent salary increment and no increase in benefits.

She worried about many aspects of a strike. She was concerned about nontenured teachers who could be thrown to the wolves if they participated. She also worried about women with husbands who might "forbid such nonsense." Would these women stick up for their rights? And how about their members who have one income and six kids to support? What if the strike should go on for months? Could all members survive financially for that long? And what about the climate down town? Would the dissension last for a long time? Finally and most important, what about the children? Could they understand? How much would their lives and their education be interrupted? How upset would little children be, and how divided would loyalties be among older students? Finally, would the damaged school/community climate ever be the same again?

"No one wants to strike," said her father, "but I don't think the town of Miller wants a poor education system either. We need good teachers, and we won't get them if the salaries here don't match other schools."

"Thanks, Dad," she said as she started for her bedroom. She was sure it would be a restless night. It was. Algot Sorenson, a school board member and a leader of the 2 percent advocates appeared in her dreams, pointing his index finger and saying, "You teachers don't know when you are well-off."

Addie scheduled the first meeting of the Miller Education Association after the first day of classes.

Hal Jamison waved to Addie as he sauntered in. He had run against her for the office of president, but told Addie he was glad she had won. He had served on negotiations for two years and now volunteered to act as chief negotiator, for which Addie was thankful. She admired his expertise with figures as well as his courage to speak up for what he believed.

The auditorium was buzzing with voices. Coming in the door was a habitually late faculty member, so Addie knew it was time to begin the meeting. Although she had given many speeches to crowds of people, she felt uncomfortable in front of her peers. She took a deep breath, banged the gavel, and began. "On behalf of the officers of the Miller Education Association, I would like to welcome you this afternoon to our first meeting of the year. This will be an organizational meeting to get you to know your committees and, hopefully, to encourage you to join one of them. We'll start with the Committee for Teachers' Rights, which will be headed by Barrett Hedlund. He would like a few words."

Barrett Hedlund, attractively thirty-ish, was a physical education instructor and track coach. He looked uncomfortable but looked directly at his colleagues as he spoke. "I'm taking the chairmanship of this committee because last year, I discovered its importance through my own personal experience," he said. "You may remember, in fact, I suppose you will never forget, that I was accused of fondling a ninth grade girl in my physical education class. Now, I don't even pretend to know why the administration believed her instead of me, but they did. Thank God, the Teachers' Rights Committee believed me. After I passed a lie detector test, our school counselor interrogated the girl again. She admitted she had grossly exaggerated the situation and that I had touched only her shoulders and her waist, and nothing else, to show her the steps in an ethnic dance." His voice broke as he said, "I almost lost my wife."

He left the podium, seemingly relieved. After a heavy moment of silence, applause roared in support of a colleague still hurting.

Public relations was under the chairmanship of Marilyn Horn, an English teacher of great note. She told of plans to bring students downtown to perform outside or wherever they could accommodate the students inside the stores.

"If the mountain won't come to Mohammed, then Mohammed must go to the mountain." she said. The audience laughed and applauded. She continued her presentation by saying, "We have a big bus scheduled to take us downtown, so meet with your committees and decide what you want to present. Come along with us. We need your help."

"Marilyn is right," Addie said. "Our committee can't do the job alone, not when we're experiencing political unrest, the Hippie Movement, and a fast moving drug culture. Also, the schools are adding more subjects and responsibilities." She paused, then spoke with conviction, "You know as well as I do that we're getting much more criticism and blame. We need to unite and work for communication that can dispel the misconceptions that promote these feelings. That is the mission of this committee."

After reports from other committees, Addie glanced at her notes and said, "I'd like to comment briefly on our membership. I hope all of you have joined our association so that we don't have to worry about losing any of you to the teachers' union. Our association is very strong, and its strength lies in committees such as the ones you have just heard from. They will work to provide a system that will insure good working conditions, attract good teachers, and offers equitable salaries."

The teachers clapped and cheered. Addie was about to adjourn the meeting when a new faculty member rose to speak.

"Madam Chairman, how long have local teachers' associations been active?"

"It's hard to say. Some began as teachers' social functions where they discussed problems but had no formal agenda."

"When was the Miller one started?"

"I'm not sure, perhaps in the late 50s."

"Wouldn't it be in your records?"

"Yes, I would think so."

"Shouldn't you have them at your fingertips?"

Realizing she was being taunted for the purpose of degrading her leadership, she asked, "What is your name?"

"Joe Gresham."

"Mr. Gresham, are you a member of this organization?"

"No."

"Then why are you here?"

"Just to visit and to see what is going on."

"Are you a union member?"

"Yes."

"Then this meeting is not open to you. This meeting is for local association members only, so I will have to ask you to leave."

He left and the group applauded, making Addie feel like a fearless leader.

The third week in September was American Education Week. Addie and the Public Relations Committee met to explore ways to improve parent visitation numbers at the schools during this week. As one elementary school teacher stated, "Visitation is an excellent idea, Addie, but the minute the visitors appear, children become so excited that it is impossible to have a normal class experience."

Addie agreed as she maneuvered her music cart, which contained rhythm instruments, bells, and charts to the first grade room, helped by Cory McNally, a first grader who was so intellectually gifted that his scores were off the charts.

"Grandpa, look what I'm doing," he called to his grandfather as they moved into the hallway.

To Addie, he added, "I'm so glad that my grandpa could come to school and watch how good I can move the music cart."

The elderly gentleman, wearing blue jeans, a plaid shirt, and a cowboy hat, introduced himself. "I'm Robert McNally, Cory's

Grandpa," he said. As they shook hands, they both laughed, for Addie immediately recognized him as the "courtesy of the road man" who had changed her tire, and he realized that she was the owner of the jack still resting in his trunk.

After apologizing profusely, Mr. McNally said, "I'm awfully glad I found you... Yesiree. I'll leave the jack in the school office before I go, and I hope you'll have a wonderful day because you teachers do a terrific job. I have two grandchildren who have gone through this system." With a beaming smile he continued, "And now, there's Cory."

Cory, eager to get back to class, pulled his grandfather away, but Mr. McNally looked back and called, "Cory will be president someday."

Smiling, Addie nodded and waved goodbye. The school day was almost over, and she needed to get on the bus to take her children's choir downtown to perform outside in front of the First National Bank.

As she entered the bus, Addie cringed at the magnitude of the sound of the high-pitched voices—fifty children from grades 3 to 6. The choir, well-behaved at rehearsals, was actively "out of school."

Knowing how difficult it would be to get their attention, Addie took a small hand drum from the bag of instruments she had brought for the concert. She often used the drum in class to develop rhythm skills. She would play a rhythm pattern in four beats that the children, without missing a beat, would repeat by clapping it. They were so attuned to the procedure that they would automatically repeat whatever pattern she played, then silently await her direction. Today was no exception—on cue, they repeated her pattern and were ready to listen.

"I'm happy that so many of you are here today," she began, "and I know that you will be wonderful representatives of our school. We want to make a good impression on the audience because...well, after all, they pay the taxes that help our schools to provide the things that we need and enjoy. This is one way we can say 'thank you.'" Then she cautioned, "Another thing, your program does not begin when you are standing outside in your choir positions in front of the bank. People will be watching you as you come down the first step of this bus. We have only five quiet blocks to go and then I'll quietly lead you off."

The children followed the directions. They quietly descended the bus steps without pushing or shoving and followed Addie to the front section outside of the bank. They sang well and brought many smiles to the audience. Addie was pleased with their performance.

On the way back to the bus, however, she pursed her lips tightly to keep from laughing as she watched two of the youngest charmers smile sweetly at the audience and say, "Thank you very much for the taxes."

Negotiations had begun in September with only two negotiators. Hal Jamison, who had two years of experience on the committee, recruited Harry Jacobs, a mathematics teacher, to serve on the committee with him.

We need more help, thought Addie one evening as she sat in her apartment, desperately combing the association list for prospects. She called two of them. Both answered with the usually fatal "I'll have to think it over" response. She suggested they ponder it fast because they were running out of thinking time.

Her search was interrupted by the sound of the doorbell. Answering her door, she was shocked to see Joe Gresham, the union irritant, smiling at her.

"Come in," she said. "Sit down. I've just made some fresh coffee." As she poured his coffee, she wondered why she was being so nice.

"So," she said, sitting opposite him, "I'm curious as to why you're here." Laughing she reminded him that this wasn't union territory.

He leaned forward and said, "Addie, I came to apologize. I'm not sure what came over me at the meeting. I've thought a lot about it. Not to excuse it, but I think I was trying to punish my ex-wife. You were the closest aim."

"But why punish her?" asked Addie, passing a plate of oatmeal cookies.

"She left me a year ago. The divorce was finalized the day of your association meeting, and she was married again that evening."

He laughed nervously. "The irony of it is that she left me because she said I never had time for her, that I buried myself in my school work and union activities. Now she's gone, and I have the time. I joined the association this morning, but I need some involvement."

When Addie asked him about negotiation experience, he revealed he had negotiated for five years and was president of his union for three years. When he asked her if he could negotiate for Miller, Addie was ecstatic.

"Joe Gresham, you are a godsend. I'll call Hal and tell him that you'll help. He just called me and said that Algot Sorenson will be replacing Clark Mills on the Board's negotiating committee. Algot has a lot of influence in the community, and I'm sure he will be head of the '2 Percent club.' Mill's company is sending him to Europe for a month or two to work on sales. I was afraid that could happen. Think you can handle Algot?"

"I'm looking forward to meeting a man who has so much clout in the community. We can probably learn something from him."

As he rose to leave, Addie was surprised at his height. He must be six feet tall, she thought. He was a handsome man with dark curly hair and brown eyes.

Walking to the door, he said, "I have to confess, Addie, that I did want to form a union here and downgrade the association. I'm sorry."

"What made you change your mind?"

"One thing was Barrett Hedlund, because I thought, we're all at risk and Lord knows we can't afford to pay the legal costs if the school shouldn't support us. Look at what happened to Barrett only last year. Any of us could find ourselves in situations where we need help, and both unions and associations provide assistance. It's a matter of choice."

"Agreed," said Addie as they shook hands and said goodnight.

Addie went to bed early and dreamed of a strike. The town lifted Algot on its shoulders.

Algot looked down at Joe, who said, "Please, let's keep trying. Maybe we can work it out."

As negotiations continued, Addie realized her dream about a strike had a strong possibility of happening. The Board and Negotiating Committee, which had met in September and October, were stuck at a 2 percent increment with no consideration of payment for two extra work days and no offer of increased benefits.

"We can't accept it," said Hal. "Right now, we're far below the towns around us, and every negotiation period seems to set us back more. We can't get further behind."

"We may have to stand and be counted," responded Joe.

"Meaning?" asked Harry.

No one answered, for it was a question to which they all knew the answer but didn't want to verbalize it.

"We are in strike climate, Addie," said Hal sadly. "I think you'll have to go to the association soon."

Addie agreed. She rose early the next morning to check the calendar and plan the association meeting for four o'clock. She opened the meeting by thanking everyone for attending on such a short notice, then called on Hal Jamison.

"I know most of you," he began, "because this is my third year of negotiating for you." The teachers applauded in appreciation. "But this year," he continued, "has been the most difficult one I have experienced. We are going no place. The Board wants to add two work days with a total salary increment of only 2 percent and no increased benefits." Groans engulfed the auditorium. "We're asking for a 10 percent increase," he said. "Now for some of you that is too much, but keep in mind, we have to play the game. The Board knows they won't give 10 percent, and we know the Board has to come up from 2 percent. Within that range, there is negotiation room. Other schools are settling for 3 percent and 4 percent, but please remember that we have two additional workdays to consider."

She worried about the outcome of the negotiations. To her, the whole process was like a checker game coming to life. First they moved, then the Board moved—back and forth—until a winner could be declared.

The next weeks were both frantic and fearful. State association leaders urged the negotiators to "stay the course," and if no agreement had been reached by November 14, they should file an Intent to Strike.

The November 13 meeting between the Board and Negotiating Committee was serious but cordial. It was over in an hour. The Board moved up to 3 percent, and the teachers moved down to 7 percent. The groups departed after refusing to move forward to an increment agreement and pay for two additional work days as well as increased benefits.

The teachers met again the following afternoon.

"We're at an impasse," reported Hal after reviewing the negotiating steps that had been taken. "We have tried our best to negotiate a realistic agreement. The final offer of the Board is 3 percent with no added benefits or pay for additional work days. Therefore, I move that we reject the Board's offer and file an Intent to Strike.   T h e strike will begin on November 20, unless an agreement is reached with the Board before that time."

The teachers voted quickly. Few hesitated. The ballots were tabulated, and the Intent to Strike vote passed, 104–14. The announcement did not stimulate any applause, and the usual bubbly conversation of the teachers was missing as they quietly left the auditorium.

The six days before the November 20 strike date were difficult. The Board and the Negotiating Committee met twice, but the impasse was not broken, and the strike was now a reality.

By eight o'clock on the first day of the strike, all teachers assigned to the morning shift were there.

The day went by slowly. Only a few townspeople came to observe. Some honked their horns as they drove past the school. Some motorists offered encouragement, others gave them "thumbs down." Teachers in four shifts kept the march going from 8:00 a.m. to 8:00 p.m. Addie took the morning shift and also filled in toward dusk. She had often wondered how it would feel to be marching for a cause, but to her surprise, she seemed devoid of any feeling except the necessity to focus ahead and keep marching without paying any attention to hecklers or other disturbances.

Following the next board meeting the local association convened, but there were no smiles from the negotiating committee. As Hal approached the podium, silence prevailed.

Without preparatory remarks he stated, "The board has offered 4 percent." Some started to applaud. Hal silenced them. "Some area schools are settling at 4 percent, but they are settling with increased benefits and no added calendar work days. Our Board has refused to increase benefits and has added two days of work with no pay, so my recommendation is to refuse their offer. Remember that the Board has the money and people want their kids back in school. They want their lives to return to normal...but 4 percent will not do the job."

A tired, upset faculty voted 90–35 to reject the offer.

The strike dragged on, and Addie divided her worries between the strike and Ben. Each day brought new problems with the strike as well as continuous worries about her relationship with Ben. She tried not to worry about the possibility of Ben and Sue's friendship turning to love, but felt some comfort in the fact that Ben had never relayed that message. She trusted him and felt he would always honor their pact, but she needed assurance that their relationship was still very strong.

By the middle of the third week, the weather was cold with hints of snow in the air, and some of the teachers failed to show up at their designated times. Addie hurried to find replacements, not wanting the community to realize that the teachers were tired and vulnerable. "Hang in there!" called Joe Gresham. "Rome wasn't built in a day, you know." His cheerfulness failed to get a good response. Fatigue and disillusionment blossomed in the cold, uncomfortable weather.

Addie's usual buoyant spirits sagged from loss of sleep and worry about the outcome. Toward the end of the week, she drove to the bakery to get some extra-special homemade doughnuts she hoped would lift spirits. Returning to the school, she was met by Marilyn, who seemed very excited.

"Addie, who is that man?"

"What man?"

"The tall guy with the dark coat and plaid cap. Do you know him?"

"I don't know," replied Addie, "but I'll find out."

Five steps farther, she knew it was Ben. She was speechless. In the cold autumn air, she hugged him and didn't want to let go. The fatigue from the long hours, responsibilities, and worries seemed to dissipate into tears of happiness as he told her he wanted to support her efforts with the strike.

Presenting him to the group, she said, "This is Ben O'Reilly, my good friend from Roseland. He just told me that fifteen faculty members from Roseland have volunteered to be here tomorrow morning. Be sure to join them. Spread the word to the rest of the faculty because it's very important to have a good turnout tomorrow, even if it is Saturday."

"Don't give up," said Ben. "In addition to the fifteen teachers from Roseland, there will be others from surrounding towns. It will be an impressive solidarity march that will be covered by the press."

Cheers struck the crisp air with an intensity that seemed to buoy spirits and raise hopes on the cold, windy day.

Addie and Ben marched together, conversing about mutual friends from Roseland. Speaking quietly, Ben asked, "Addie, can we leave for a few minutes and talk privately? I don't have much time because I have to meet with the Rotary committee this afternoon in Minneapolis."

"Sure. We'll go to my place. I need to phone three more marchers for the afternoon shift anyway, and it's close enough to walk."

As they entered Addie's apartment, Ben admired the new drapes and coffee table.

"You haven't seen them before?" quizzed Addie. "It is a long time since you were here."

"I'm sorry it didn't work out better, Addie."

She braced herself, feeling that the next words might be about Sue or about her note expressing the need for a talk; but she was surprised to hear him ask, "Addie, what are you doing for Christmas?"

"I'll be home. What about you?"

"I'll be there, too." He laughed, adding, "If I'm invited, of course."

"Of course you're invited, Ben. With the strike going on, I haven't even thought about Christmas, but your coming will help me get started. Can you come for Christmas Eve? How long can you stay?"

"Just Christmas Eve and Christmas Day. Our office is crazy this time of year with the tax season on the horizon."

Fishing for information she asked, "Do you have many Christmas parties in the offing?"

"Just an office party and a couple at church."

Thoughts of Ben and Sue emerged, but she dismissed them quickly and made her calls while Ben read the paper.

As they walked back, he said, "I'm looking forward to Christmas."

"I am too, Ben," she said as she reached for his hug.

Addie rejoined the marchers. Ben waved goodbye to the group and was soon just a distant speck down the highway.

At ten o'clock the next morning, sixty local teachers and thirty from area schools marched in the strike. Townspeople came to watch. Some showed support, some expressed disappointment, some were noncommunicative. The day was long, but finally over. The strikers, looking weary, left the school grounds.

In the middle of the following week, the Board called a meeting. Addie called an association meeting the following day at which Hal briskly approached the podium with a smile, shouting, "Good news! We have been offered 5 percent."

Wild applause and whistles filled the room. "How about benefits?" asked Marilyn.

"No improvement, but I think we can live without a benefits change this year. We'll work for them next year. Therefore, I move that we accept the school board's proposal."

The motion passed unanimously. The teachers were tired. The community was tired. The strike was over.

Chapter 9

CHANGES

The weeks before Christmas were busy ones for Addie at the farm. Gradually, the tension from the strike and its aftermath decreased, and Addie's sleep patterns improved. School was released only two days before Christmas, giving her little time to prepare for the holidays.

She eagerly awaited Ben's arrival on Christmas Eve. In a holiday letter, Estelle mentioned that Sue and her family were spending Christmas in Ireland. The news caused her to wonder if Ben would have spent the holidays with them, had they been available. Before Sue entered the picture, she would worry only about Catholic-Lutheran differences. Now, her worries were enlarged by Sue's involvement in Ben's life. The internal bantering continued even after Ben arrived at the farm. She felt a tinge of concern when he guided her to the couch.

Then, abruptly Ben said, "Addie, I want to do this while we're alone."

"Do what?"

"Ask you to marry me. I know the religious differences aren't solved yet, but we'll do it together. I don't want to sit year after year thinking, 'What are we going to do?'" His voice cracked as he said, "I love you, Addie, and I want you to marry me."

Addie looked at him in wonderment. She couldn't find words, but her thoughts were racing. Was it actually happening? This can't be a dream, can it? No, no, it's real. It must be real.

Finally finding her voice, she answered, "I love you too, Ben. I love you so much that there were a few times when I was almost glad for a strike to take my mind off worrying about your relationship with Sue…because more than anything, I've always wanted to be your wife."

"Sue and I worked together in church and attended some movies together," said Ben. "It turned out to be just friendship, but I wanted to give it a chance to see if I could stop thinking about you. She's a wonderful person, but she isn't you, Addie. And no one can take your place," he whispered. "Now I know it."

Addie's tears flowed. Ben laughed as he dried them, saying, "I'll have to get used to those 'happiness tears.'"

He took out a small box and put a diamond ring on her finger. "I believe they call this an engagement ring," he said.

"Whatever they call it, I'll treasure it."

Their lingering kiss was interrupted by Addie's father's footsteps, indicating the nap was over. Seeing the diamond, he embraced them both. The happiness in her father's eyes made Addie's circle of joy complete.

The opening of Christmas gifts continued the evening's excitement. Addie had bought gold cuff links for Ben.

"Great," he said with a smile. "I'll wear them at a wedding that's coming up."

"When will it be?" asked her father.

"I guess we haven't decided," answered Ben. "Addie, speak your piece."

She was silent for so long that he inquired, "You haven't changed your mind, have you? I'm getting nervous."

She laughed and answered, "Of course not," but inquired if he remembered that she told him she had applied for a position in Nigeria.

"Sure," he replied. "Beginning in July you would be an exchange teacher for six weeks in one of their Christian schools, and you would also work on their testing program."

"Right. Dad knows about the latest development, but I haven't had time until now to tell you that yesterday I received a letter accepting me for the position."

She paused, then asked, "Do you suppose we could have the wedding in August, or should we get married before I go?"

"Before you go," he said. "How about a June wedding?"

"Fine. The twentieth of June would be all right if it works for you. It's my parent's anniversary." She smiled at her father.

Looking at the calendar, she joked, "Look, Ben, June 20th is on a Saturday. You don't work, so you could come."

"Well, I guess," he answered, smiling; but when she asked where he wanted to go, and he answered "Nigeria," the bantering stopped.

"Are you saying you could go with me to Nigeria for six weeks?" she asked.

He answered affirmatively, explaining that he didn't take a vacation last year, he had the time coming, and he knew that Lyle could hold down the fort.

"I didn't think I could ever be happier than I was a few minutes ago when you gave me the ring," said Addie, "but now you have added another dimension. "I love you, Ben O'Reilly."

January was a cold, lonesome month with bad roads and difficult travel, but Addie's happiness warmed many relationships. Even Algot Sorenson responded to her spirited remarks.

Entering his store, she praised his after Christmas sale items. Addie often bought birthday gifts at these sales, and this day was no exception.

As he wrapped her gifts, he thanked her, saying, "Addie, I'm so glad the strike is over."

Concurring, she added, "We'll have to work hard to rebuild trust."

"Right," answered Algot.

They shook hands, then Addie smiled and left.

The long winter also gave Addie a chance to reminisce with her father, remembering earlier days, especially those with her mother.

"Remember, Dad, when she complained to the school about their scheduling special music groups after school when bus kids couldn't come, and how it got changed in a hurry?"

"She was really upset," he answered. "If she had lived a little earlier, she would have been right beside Susan B. Anthony, agitating for women's rights."

"Really, Dad?"

"She believed in helping the underdog, like in the gospel of the sparrow. She lived it, you know."

"I know," acknowledged Addie.

On warm days, Addie enjoyed cross-country skiing. As she glided along, she remembered the ski trails she and her cousin, Cynthia, would travel. They lived two miles apart. Sometimes they would each ski one mile and meet halfway from their homes before going to either Addie's or Cynthia's house, depending on whose mother had been doing the most baking.

Turning right by a neighbor's shed, she noticed a large straw pile covered with snow. It reminded her of an experience from her childhood that she usually tried to push back into the irretrievable part of her memory, but it never worked. She remembered the beautiful winter day she went skiing with Aaron, an older cousin, who would always tease her by calling her "Skinny Legs."

"Skinny Legs," he would yell, "see if you can stand up going down this straw pile. Come on, Skinny Legs!"

Finally, overcome by his taunting, she said, "Okay, Aaron. I'm coming up."

She made her way to the top of the straw pile, but instead of skiing down herself, she pushed him. Aaron, unprepared for descent, fell down the hill, and lay at the bottom, crying. He had a sprained ankle, but Addie had a broken heart and could remember the exact words of her tearful apology.

"I'm so sorry, Aaron. I don't know why I did it. Well, I guess I do. It was because you kept calling me 'Skinny Legs,' but I shouldn't have pushed you. Can you forgive me?"

He answered gruffly, "Well, I 'spose." Aaron walked on crutches for two weeks. Whenever anyone asked him how it happened, he seemed to enjoy removing Addie from her pedestal by saying, "'Miss Perfect' pushed me down a straw pile."

Addie remembered that her folks thought she had punished herself more than anyone else could, so they discussed self-control and resumed normal living.

Though the winter continued bleak and cold, Addie was happy. Life was good, she thought. She was engaged to the man she loved and was secure in her belief that they could deal with any roadblock that might threaten their happiness. Documents from the Vatican Council had been promulgated and permission secured from the Bishop to be married in Addie's church. Father O'Malley and Pastor Lee would share the service.

At a Sunday dinner with Joe and Verona as guests, she revealed some of her plans. "Verona, will you be my maid of honor?" she asked. "I'd like to have you and Ginny and my high school friend Marcia as attendants. Estelle said she would sing, and my cousin Cynthia and her husband will be the host couple."

"I'd be honored," answered Verona, who was looking happier than she had for a long time. She and Joe Gresham had begun dating during the strike and were together frequently. Joe's two-year-old boy adored Verona and would often snuggle into her arms, looking content and happy. As Addie watched them, she wondered if she would ever have the blessing of a baby.

Having Ben's child would bring more happiness than she could even contemplate. A visit to the doctor, however, confirmed her fears of possibly not being able to conceive.

"It's not for sure, Addie," he said. "Maybe you'll surprise me."

She fought back tears as she wrote Ben, who answered promptly, writing, "As long as our lives are joined, I know I'll be happy with or without a genetic child. Relax, Addie. We'll deal with it together. P.S. Remember the Sparrow."

The letter soothed her, and she smiled at the postscript. They would hold up the sky together, she thought happily. At bedtime, she read the letter again before turning out the lights and praying that God would bless them with a child according to His will.

The nineteenth of June, the day of the groom's dinner, was cold and rainy, but the joy of the occasion warmed her as much as a comforting summer sun.

Ginny had driven from Peoria with her two daughters, five-year-old Pattie and little Addie. Hank, who was speaking at a convention in Chicago, would fly in the next day in time for the wedding, which was scheduled for 2:00 p.m.

Ginny's excitement of seeing Addie intensified as they reached Addie's street and were soon at her house.

Addie screamed her welcome as Ginny and the girls entered her home. Ginny, who was laughing and crying intermittently, hugged Addie and said, "I'm so glad to see you and so happy for you. Tell me all about him."

Shortly after enjoying reminiscences, they heard a scream from the room where the children were playing.

"Our little princess is getting tired," Ginny said as she rescued the tiny crawler from the clutches of her older sibling. Addie lifted her little namesake into her arms and comforted her by drying her eyes and holding her close.

It had been a long day for Ginny and her daughters, so they left for the hotel to rest before dinner. Addie decided to do the same, but her plans were interrupted by the doorbell. She opened it and was surprised to see Marcia smiling and holding out her arms to embrace her.

"Marcia, I'm so glad to see you," said Addie. Peering over Marcia's shoulder, she added, "It looks like you're driving a Buick now. Whatever happened to the 1938 Chevrolet?"

"Addie, I think you and I enjoyed most of its last wonderful miles."

"I appreciated every one of them," said Addie as she led her friend into the living room to a comfortable chair.

"We had such fun in that car discussing our futures and making plans," said Marcia. "I know you were determined to have both a marriage and a career; and now it's happening according to plans."

"And you wanted to marry Les as soon as possible, be a good wife, have children and live happily ever after on the farm. Seems like it turned out well, Marcia."

"It's never perfect, but Les and I are good together, and he is great at holding up the sky, but he just couldn't do it when our three-year-old daughter's kidneys shutdown."

"I was so sorry to hear about her death," said Addie softly.

"It was very difficult to accept, but you and many others held up the sky for us when we couldn't do it ourselves. The next year, as you remember, was the year we were blessed with little twin boys. They're in junior high school now. They remember your visits and are excited about coming to your wedding."

"I'll be excited to see them too," said Addie.

The conversation moved from "catch-up" to talk of the bank and the egg station. They munched on chocolate drops from Thor's stash as the afternoon slipped away.

Marcia looked at her watch and stood up quickly, exclaiming, "It's just like old times. Time goes so fast when we're together, but today, I left Les at the John Deere garage, and I was supposed to pick him up a half hour ago."

"I'll walk with you to your car."

They walked slowly, not speaking, but absorbed in thoughts triggered by their visit.

As Marcia stepped into the car and rolled down the window, Addie laughed and said, "I love your car, Marcia, but I guess I am still partial to the 1938 Chevrolet."

"I guess I am too," replied Marcia. "It gave us both a great ride into the future."

The groom's dinner was held at six o'clock at the Whitford Prairie Café. When everyone had arrived, they sat down to enjoy steaks, hors d'oeuvres, fresh pumpernickel bread, and a delectable array of salads.

"Great food," said Michael O'Reilly as he stood to make a toast. "I'd like to toast a wonderful couple," he began. "My kid brother, who I've always admired, and a beautiful girl named Addie, who I've heard about for over five years, are going to be married." He looked directly at them. "I really began to worry that you two might never make it to the altar, but I'm happy that tomorrow you will. I wish you all the happiness life can offer."

Following the toasts, the entourage made their way to the church for rehearsal. Father O'Malley and Pastor Lee seemed to have everything under control. Addie looked at Ben, who was holding his four-year-old nephew, Nathan, in his arms. Addie had met Michael and his wife, Crystal, only once, but she had been impressed with their warm and welcoming spirit. Nathan would be the ring bearer, and Ginny's five-year-old daughter, Pattie, would be the flower girl. As Addie gazed at Ben and Nathan, she offered another silent prayer. Maybe praying in church will help, she thought, then laughed at the ludicrous notions she could entertain regarding an all powerful God. She changed her prayer to a plea for forgiveness, then turned her thoughts to Pastor Lee's directions.

By 8:00 p.m. the rehearsal was over, and everyone had left the church. Addie and her father returned home.

She suggested having a cup of coffee, but tea would be more sleep inducing. Thor looked at his daughter fondly. "It's been a long time since Oscar."

"Oscar? Oh, my pet lamb. Whatever made you think of him?"

"I don't know. Maybe because I think of lambs as being so little and unwary. Even if you're old enough to face your problems alone, I still think of you as my 'little girl.' But, tomorrow I give you away. I'm glad it's to Ben."

"Dad, he wants you to come and live with us. Of course, I do too!"

"Do I look that fragile?" asked Thor, standing up as tall and strong as he could.

"No, but I think you're standing on your toes," said Addie, laughing.

"No, Addie, this is your life. I'll be fine here. I was going to tell you that I ran into Verona the other day when I went to Miller for some machinery parts. On the spur of the moment, I asked her if she would consider working for me the rest of the summer. She agreed to cook for the hired man and me and to look after the garden."

Addie looked at him in amazement.

"Never underestimate your elders," she said, embracing him. "That's great, Dad. That's just great."

The day of the wedding was beautiful. Addie rose early and took her coffee to the picnic table outside. The dew was still on the grass and butterflies were flying from flower to flower. The air was still, its quietness penetrated only by the chirping of the birds and the steady beat of a red-headed woodpecker.

Addie had always enjoyed these mornings. She would miss filling the bird feeder and watching different birds come to eat. She had begun to think of them as her own special aviary.

To her surprise, her father came out to join her. "Couldn't you sleep?" she asked.

"Thought I'd get up and rehearse that fancy step that I do with you when we walk to the altar."

"You are reputed to be one of the finest dancers in the county, and you're worrying about a simple step like that? Come on, Dad."

"No, I just wanted to come out to wish you well while I have you alone. I probably won't get a chance at the church, you know, with so many people."

"I know, Dad, but I'd know how you feel even if you didn't get a chance to say it."

"But I want to say it, Addie. I've never been good at words, but I wanted to tell you how happy I am for you."

She looked at the intense expression on his face and the love in his eyes, this man who had given her so much and had provided such a stellar role model for her life. Both she and her father knew that this was their personal goodbye to life as it had been. As Addie watched him start down the road for his daily walk, she saw him take out his handkerchief. She was tearful also, but her emotions were mixed with tears of sadness for the separation and tears of joy for the coming union.

Addie dressed and drove into town to meet Ginny. They checked the flowers and food arrangements to be sure that everything would go smoothly, then met Estelle at the local diner for brunch.

By 1:30 p.m., the guests were filing into the church. Shortly before 2:00 p.m., Addie's father knocked on the door to Addie's dressing room. When she opened it, he could only stare at his daughter who was dressed in a white lace-fitted gown that accentuated her figure. Her hair was in an upsweep, capped by the lace veil her mother had worn thirty-five years ago.

Thor bowed and asked her if she would like to go for a walk. "Sure, Dad, I've been ready for this walk for a few years."

"You look beautiful, Addie. You look a lot like your mother."

As they approached the entrance, they saw Marcia trying to separate Pattie from little Nathan, who wanted some of Pattie's flowers. The music was cueing Marcia to enter, and she was frantic. Just then, Cynthia came bounding up the stairs to help. Marcia, smoothing her lavender gown, entered a little late as Ginny, dressed in soft beige, was already at the altar. Verona, coming up the stairs just before Addie and her father, was the last attendant to enter. She wore a pale pink dress identical to the others in style. All three carried pink and white roses.

The volume of the music heightened, indicating it was time for Addie to make her entrance. She smiled at her father as he held out his arm.

Entering the church, her first glance went toward Ben, whose broad smile seemed to invite her to hurry and join him, and whose eyes never wavered from her. He and his attendants wore pink shirts and ties and burgundy tuxedos. They looked handsome, thought Addie. She wondered if Ben were as happy as she. She wondered if anyone could be.

As she walked down the aisle, she was radiant, enjoying each step of the way. She had a strange sensation that her mother was on the other side of her, that she was being escorted by both parents. She could almost feel her mother saying, "This is the crown, Addie. Enjoy it!"

As they reached the altar, Thor gave Addie's arm to Ben, who whispered, "You're so beautiful."

Estelle stood to sing "Oh Promise Me." Her voice filled the church with its rich tones. Then, without hesitation, the organist played the introduction to another piece, one unknown to Addie.

"What is she playing?" whispered Addie. "I don't remember choosing that music."

"I don't know it," answered Ben.

Father O'Malley smiled as Estelle sailed effortlessly into a song about sparrows building a house of love. The refrain echoed "Remember the Sparrow."

Addie was overcome. Only Estelle could do this, she thought. "I'm sure she composed it."

She looked at Ben, the man who would soon be her husband. He mouthed, "Don't cry," but she noted that his eyes looked moist. Addie, however, did not cry. Her happiness had reached such a buoyancy that she wanted to run across the room to embrace each guest and tell them to share her wonderful feeling of joy. Her thoughts returned to earth just in time for the exchange of vows and pronouncement of their union. The recessional was joyous; the ceremony was over.

Ben, Addie, Thor, and Michael and Crystal O'Reilly formed the reception line. Because it was so short, guests engaged the five in longer conversations, but after an hour of standing and smiling, Addie told Ben, "I can't stand these heels a minute longer" and kicked them off.

"I saw you, Addie O'Reilly." She recognized Hank's voice, telling her she looked beautiful, even without shoes.

Ben put his arm around her and led her to a chair.

"Rest, dear," he said. "I'll bring you some punch. We'll eat, take just a few more pictures and be off to Nigeria."

Addie smiled.

The Prairie Café catered the refreshments—strawberry punch, chicken salad, buns, fruits, and wedding cake. After the meal and pictures, Ben and Addie changed into street clothes. Addie wore a new light blue suit that matched the color of her eyes. Her blonde hair was still in an upsweep, crowned with the tiara, from her veil. Ben, freed from the tuxedo, looked comfortable in a dark suit.

Through a shower of rice, they waved goodbye to the guests and sped to Minneapolis to catch an early flight to a distant, different land.

Chapter 10

NIGERIA

From the air, the African villages looked peaceful with sprawling mud-block buildings and green jungle dotting the landscape. As they landed on African soil, they felt the incomparable difference between the country they had left and the strange new land they were visiting. People milled around quietly, socializing with neighbors. Moslem women were dressed in brightly colored cloth, from which they fashioned blouses and skirts. The men wore caps and light-colored robes over loose pants.

Ben called for a cab to take them to the school. The cab, which was black, appeared to be very old, but meticulously clean. They laughed at the sign on the car. In white paint, it read, "Unpaid Debts."

"Do all cabs have signs or slogans?" asked Ben.

"No, just the creative ones," said the driver, laughing.

Soon they pulled up to the Christian school, a drab gray building made of mud blocks with a corrugated tin roof.

"I imagine the tin is needed to protect the mud blocks from the rain," said Ben as he helped Addie out of the cab. "They have enormous rainfalls here."

But today, the air was dry and gentle, and the quietness was broken only by vividly colored birds singing to the world, accompanied by the smell of onions and spices.

"Wonder what they're cooking," said Ben, stepping out of the cab and giving Addie his hand. Their observations were interrupted by a smiling, middle-aged man who came out to meet them.

"I assume that you are the O'Reillys," he said. "I'm Mr. Abiola, the principal. We are most happy, Mrs. O'Reilly, to have you come and work with us. We welcome you, Mr. O'Reilly, as well. Come in and see the school. Then I will take you to your living quarters." Except for his dark skin and perfect English, he reminded Addie of the superintendent from Miller.

"We are in need of new facilities, but we can't get them yet," said Mr. Abiola.

And that's just like home, thought Addie.

"You will have classes every morning for three hours," continued Mr. Abiola. "Your afternoons will be spent on preparations and on assessing tests given yearly by the West African Examination Council."

He escorted them into a large classroom that housed five narrow tables with benches for seating.

"You will have twenty students. There will be four students at each table."

Addie was relieved to find that she had a desk with a straight back chair, and that on the wall, above her desk, was a world map.

The living quarters were adjacent to the school. The large mud-block home contained three bedrooms, a kitchen, and a large living room. Heavy screens were fastened into the walls of the home, as were the doors. Most of the furniture, including the beds, had stained wood frames.

Straight-back chairs with upholstered seats looked comfortable and inviting.

"They must have expected a family," said Ben. "We'll have to yell to find each other here."

Wonderful place to stay, thought Addie as she thought of its contrast to the simple classroom.

The bathroom had a sink, tub, and toilet, while the half-bath contained a shower and small sink. Water, on a tilted floor, drained from the shower to a cement pipe close to the floor, which directed the water to the outside. It was plugged when not in use.

The kitchen was small, but it had a sink, a stove, and a refrigerator.

"Mr. Abiola said that the water is drinkable without being boiled," said Ben. "Look! It's pumped to a big vat on top of the house and heated by the sun during the day. Evidently, they use it in the evening. Isn't that remarkable?"

"This stove reminds me of a campfire stove," said Addie. "But where will we get gas?"

"There's a Petrol station close by," answered Ben, as he pointed to a sign advertising it.

"Ben, look!" Addie said, peering out her kitchen window. "We have a garden, and even a bird feeder." The feeder reminded her of home and her father, but the brightly colored birds flying around the feeder brought her back to Nigeria. "This is a different life, Ben."

"It's an interesting one, Addie. I'm glad we're here."

In the afternoon, they shopped for groceries for the evening meal. The market was filled with strange foods that piqued their curiosity. Finally, they chose *fufu* and *kenkey* and prepared them as they would dumplings served with a pepper sauce. They would try the lamb kebob later. Also, they would soon try the Nigerian meal of goat stew, yams, and cooking bananas called plantains.

While preparing the food, they heard a soft knock at the door. Opening it, they saw a smiling little boy with dark hair and deep brown eyes.

He can't be more than five years old, thought Addie.

"Good afternoon," intoned the visitor expressively. "Welcome to our land."

"Thank you very much," responded Addie. "And what is your name?"

"Good afternoon!" replied the boy, using even more expression. "Welcome to our land."

Kneeling down, Ben gained eye contact with the child. "Where do you live?" he asked.

"Good afternoon. Welcome to our land," repeated the smiling boy once more before waving goodbye and running out the door.

Following him outside, Ben exclaimed, "He's a neighbor. He ran into a house three doors from here."

"It was nice of him to welcome us," said Addie. "He evidently doesn't know many words in English, but he uses wonderful intonation in the words he does use."

At six o'clock that evening, they sat down to enjoy their newly found delicacies, but they were interrupted by sudden darkness. Night came with the immediacy of a bedroom shade being drawn on sunlight.

"What happened?" asked Addie.

"We're six degrees above the equator," answered Ben. "I guess, we forgot the importance of that detail."

"Thank goodness we have electricity," said Addie as she turned on the lights.

Before going to sleep, she said, "I'm nervous about tomorrow. I'm not at all sure I should have tackled this assignment."

"You'll be fine, dear. Don't doubt yourself."

Sleep was welcome, but short. They were awakened early in the morning by a burst of sunlight that came as quickly as the darkness of the night before.

"The sun certainly doesn't linger on the horizon," said Addie. "It just zooms its way right up into the heavens."

In the distance, they heard running feet and the chanting of Moslem prayers. "Go back to sleep," said Addie. "I'll see you at noon."

"I wish you could stay."

"So do I," she said, starting out the door.

Suddenly she came back. Bending down to give him a kiss she said, "But at least we had last night together before the sun zoomed into the heavens."

"You're right," Ben answered, smiling, "and it will zoom again tonight."

Addie laughed and hurried out the door where she heard a cheerful voice call, "Hello. How are you?"

"Well, I'm fine, thank you," answered Addie, "But where are you? I can't see you."

"Have a good day," the mysterious voice said.

Looking up on the roof, she laughed out loud at an African gray parrot cheerfully saying, "Goodbye."

As she entered the school room, Principal Abiola and twenty students—twelve boys and eight girls who ranged in ages, from fourteen to eighteen—stood and greeted Addie with smiles. They wore school uniforms. The girls were dressed in dark green jumpers and light green blouses; the boys wore dark green shorts and light green shirts.

"I would like to introduce a visiting faculty member to you today," said Mr. Abiola. "She is from America and is here to help you become more knowledgeable in literature and in English usage. She will be teaching the novel, Silas Marner. Please welcome Mrs. O'Reilly."

The students stood, clapped, and chorused, "Welcome."

With rapt attention, they seemed to absorb every word she uttered and to wait expectantly for more, sometimes nodding in agreement as their eyes followed her every movement.

"We'll be reading Silas Marner, an English novel by George Eliot," said Addie. "This novel was selected by the teachers in your school."

"Will it be in the final test?" asked one student.

Oh, they're normal, thought Addie.

"Will you know what the questions are, Mrs. O'Reilly?"

"Yes, I presume so."

"Please, Mrs. O'Reilly, will you be sure to cover that information?"

"Of course," answered Addie. "Now, look…" She paused as she noticed that they all leaned forward to show her they were looking very intently at her. She smiled, realizing that her use of the word *look* was confusing to them. She would have to be more careful of her own word usage.

"I hope you will read Silas Marner and work hard on it, not just for the test, but also for enjoyment."

They smiled and nodded affirmatively.

After discussing the curriculum and introducing Silas Marner, Addie looked at her watch.

The morning she had thought would move so slowly had already disappeared into noon.

When Addie arrived home, she was both surprised and pleased to find Ben making sandwiches.

"I'm discovering you're nice to have around," she said. Then she told him about the wonderful morning she had experienced with the most respectful students she had ever seen—how they stood when she entered the classroom and when they spoke in class, and if they asked her anything they would always begin their request with, "Please, Mrs. O'Reilly."

Ben was not surprised, as he felt that his young guide, Obasi, whom he had met that morning, was also impressive. He had found Obasi working in a nearby park. After talking with him, he realized the great knowledge Obasi had of his country, so he hired him. And he thought they should all have lunch one day so Addie could meet him too.

"Great," responded Addie.

"He went to a school like the one you're teaching at, Addie. He had high hopes of going to medical school and becoming a doctor, but on the day of his Sixth Form Examination to get into the university, he was very sick. He had malaria, but they told him to take the test anyway, and he missed passing it by one point."

"How terrible," acknowledged Addie. "But why didn't he repeat it?"

Ben replied that he couldn't repeat it or take it at another time or another year—that he would be forever known as a test failer even though he had always been a straight A student.

Now I can understand their concern about tests, thought Addie.

Ben had other interesting news. The "Welcome Boy" was back, he said, but he had added another word, so now the greeting was, "Welcome to our land, Nigeria."

"I hope he'll come back in the afternoon sometime," said Addie. "I'd like to see him again."

The days in the classroom were full. By the middle of the second week, the students had read Silas Marner and were ready to discuss it.

"The novel deals with some difficult circumstances and, consequently, some human failings. What are some of them?" she asked the class.

"Lying," said one. "Silas's friend said Silas had stolen money from the church. He hadn't. His friend was the guilty one."

"Loss of faith," said another. "Silas lost his faith because the church drew lots and said he was guilty of stealing from them, but he was innocent. The church wouldn't let him back unless he confessed and returned the money—money he hadn't stolen—so he left the town and went to a place called Raveloe."

"Anything else? Anybody?" asked Addie.

Finally one of the quieter young women responded, "He went from worshipping God to worshipping his gold. At night, he would count it and run it through his fingers." She smiled and continued. "A little girl crawled into his home and heart and caused him to have a spiritual rebirth. It was a wonderful ending."

The class agreed.

The following day was scheduled for review. As the students entered the classroom, one of the boys stood and asked, "Please, Mrs. O'Reilly, could we have class outside today?"

"If you can find a place for us," answered Addie.

The boy quickly led the group to a huge African oak tree. "This is one of the 'school trees' where we can have class if we wish," explained the boy.

As they sat enjoying the weather and listening to the birds, even Addie was reluctant to begin the review. Noticing a group of young children sitting under another "school tree" close by, she asked, "What do you think they are studying?"

"They're learning to read English," a girl responded.

"I'm curious," said Addie. "How do you learn it?"

"We learn it first by listening carefully to a sentence or a phrase. Then we repeat it over and over again," said one of the girls.

Like my little visitor, mused Addie before asking, "But how do you learn to read it and write it?"

"I'll show you," offered the girl as she quickly ran to the young children's "school tree" and conversed with the teacher. She returned with a chart and a color book. On the chart was printed "Today is a very nice day."

"Listen as I read the sentence," she said, using her classmates as a mock class. "Then you will repeat it exactly as I say it."

After the class had intoned it successfully, she said, "That was well done." The class smiled.

"Now, we will study the words," she said. "You will write the first word, which is *today*, on your tablet. The first letter is *T*, and I will show you a picture from the coloring book of something that starts with the letter *T*."

The class immediately identified the picture as a table and noted that it, too, began with the letter *T*, just like the word *today*.

"Now, we will study the vowel sounds," she continued. "They are the sounds that hold the letters together."

After completing a variety of exercises in vowel sounds, the young teacher concluded the lesson by saying, "That is the way I learned it when I was a little girl, but methods are not always the same."

"I learned it differently," remarked one of the boys.

"How did you learn it?" inquired Addie.

"Just the opposite. I started with the letters."

"Learning has many approaches," said Addie, "but you all speak beautiful English, and you also read it well, so the approach each of you used must have worked for you."

Glancing at her watch, she continued, "Now we will review Silas Marner. Please open your books to chapter 8."

As the class opened them, Addie groaned inwardly at the condition of the books.

"I can't compliment you on the way you take care of your books," she said. "It looks as though you were careless with them."

The class cowered at her words. They looked at each other quizzically. One girl appeared to be on the verge of tears, while the rest of the class looked at the floor as though they were accepting punishment. Finally, a boy broke the silence, "I think I should tell you that the climate here is responsible for the condition of our books," he said. "It is so moist that the pages turn up and deteriorate, and soon we cannot use them. We cannot even have a library in our school. We are sorry for the condition of our books."

Addie's shoulders sagged as she realized she had criticized them unfairly. "I'm sorry," she said. "I didn't know. Please forgive me."

Nodding their heads, they smiled at her as they began the review, but both Addie and the class were subdued. The spark was gone, and the arrival of noon was a welcome retreat from the misunderstanding.

Addie joined Ben for lunch and met Obasi, a handsome young man with olive skin and deep brown eyes.

"I hope you will enjoy your stay in our country," he said. Addie smiled and expressed her thanks.

"Do you have much going on tomorrow?" asked Ben.

"No, I have some free time then."

"Good. Obasi has invited us to go to Lagos with him. We can catch a plane and be there in an hour. Shall we go?"

"Sure. I'd like to see a little of the capital."

They rented a car at Lagos and joined in the fast moving, horn honking traffic of the industrial city.

"The traffic is just like in the cities at home," said Ben.

"Look!" said Addie. "Some people are holding umbrellas, and it isn't even raining."

"They're afraid of the monkeys," said Obasi. "Families of monkeys live up in the hills on the edge of the city. Sometimes they get loose and attack by jumping from trees on to people, so umbrellas keep them away. Notice how they also have bananas to throw into the distance in order to get the monkeys away from them."

"Interesting," said Ben, "but it certainly makes me want to stay away from trees."

As they approached a hilly area, they were surprised to see a large group of people standing and waiting.

"What is happening here, Obasi?" asked Ben.

Obasi explained that they were waiting for Mama Comfort, a medical doctor who had studied in America and returned to help her people.

Mama Comfort, a tall, handsome Nigerian woman with prominent cheekbones, came from the house, carrying her box of medical supplies. She smiled as she greeted the people.

"They come from miles around to see her," said Obasi. "She has been here for twentyfive years. She is kind and gentle, and the people trust her and love her."

As they left the hilly area, Obasi pointed out impressive buildings and historic statues.

Soon they approached a railroad roundhouse area.

"What's going on here?" asked Ben, looking at a large iron fence behind, which stood many little children who were looking out at passers-by. Some were crying.

"These are children orphaned by a civil war," said Obasi. "They are fed by the government, but they have no families or housing. Since the temperature is 80 degrees, they sleep outside, probably on mats."

They parked the car and went to the fence. Some of the tiny children were calling, "Mama. Papa."

Addie noticed Ben pausing at the end of the line to talk to one of the smallest children.

The child had light olive skin and questioning eyes. "Papa," he said, opening his arms.

The drive back to the airport was quiet—almost a penetrating silence.

At least twice a week Addie and Ben opened their home to the students. It was an opportunity to see them in a different light, away from the pressures of school. Eating Addie's chocolate chip cookies and drinking ice water, they seemed to be like most teenagers. Some giggled, some smiled shyly, some flirted, and some looked bored. Addie, recognizing her students' eagerness to learn, often went to the marketplace to buy a *Newsweek* magazine and the *New York Times*. She knew they could not afford to buy papers and magazines themselves, and she felt they needed this opportunity to expand their horizons.

As the students were sharing a *New York Times* one evening, one of the girls giggled and held up a picture of Tony Curtis.

"Look at this man," she said.

"And you look just like him," she observed, nudging the boy next to her as she spoke in soft, velvety tones.

He responded with a shy, appreciative smile, but quickly passed the paper on to the next student.

Ben also expanded the students' horizons as he talked about his duties as county auditor, president of Rotary International, his experiences in scouting and, most of all, about life in America. The boys often expressed a desire to see the country.

"How about you girls?" asked Addie.

"Oh yes," they answered.

"Good," said Addie. "You must all come and visit us."

Addie told about her life on the farm. When she talked about her pet lamb, she noticed their interest in animals.

"The lamb would pull my little red wagon," she said.

"Like a horse?" they asked, trying to visualize the scene.

"We love horses," said one of the boys, "but we don't have many here. The tsetse fly kills them. There will be a zoo in town tomorrow, though, and they'll have a horse. Please, Mrs. O'Reilly, could we go? Some of us have never seen one."

Addie rebelled inwardly at the thought of taking valuable school time to see a horse, but seeing such excitement at the mere mention of the animal, she agreed.

"I'll go too," said Ben. "I'd like to see the zoo."

The following day, Addie, Ben, and the students walked to town and stood in line with much of the rest of the populace. The line moved slowly. The students enjoyed watching the elephants and other animals, but they became very excited as they neared the scraggly looking dark brown horse.

Addie noticed that the youngest, shyest student had forged ahead of his classmates and was now very close to the animal. Listening intently, she heard the young boy who never spoke in class become very conversational with the horse.

"Hello, my name is Barima," he said. "You are such a beautiful brown color." He paused for a moment, then continued, "But you look so lonesome." As he reached out to pet the horse and stroke its mane, he said softly, "I feel that way, too."

Addie's feelings of empathy were interrupted by Ben, who had run from his post at the end of the student line to join her.

"With all the beautiful animals here," he exclaimed, "how can they get so excited about a scraggly horse?"

"I don't know," said Addie, "but I wish they could see a horse race in America. They would be so excited."

Her thoughts returned to Barima. She wondered where he had gone, but finally spotted him quite far ahead of the group.

As usual, he walked alone.

At the next social gathering at their home, Ben and Addie noticed that the students seemed unduly excited. The girls poked each other and giggled a little, and the boys looked toward the door as if they were expecting someone.

"What's going on, Ben?" asked Addie as she corralled him to the kitchen. "I have no idea. I thought maybe you had a clue."

The answer was given by Obasi, who had been invited to the party that evening and arrived carrying a tape recorder.

"Mr. and Mrs. O'Reilly," said Obasi, "the students and I would like to honor your recent marriage by performing a dance that we created for you. I'll start the music. It is a well-known folk tune."

The students rose to get into formation. Their steps were graceful and their smiles radiant. One of the girls carefully placed a wedding veil on Addie's head. Soon the bridal couple was coaxed into joining them, and with a little patient tutoring, Ben and Addie were ready to lead the procession.

Noticing that Barima was not dancing, Addie called to him, asking that he join them up front. The students, following her lead, clapped and chanted, "Barima, Barima, Barima!" until he came forward, smiling shyly at the attention he was receiving.

One section of the music seemed to motivate impromptu dance solos from those selected by the group. Soon the chant was for Barima. Addie cringed, feeling it was too much too soon, but to her surprise, Barima stepped forth. Again, he was smiling, and soon, she knew why.

His rhythm is unbelievable, she thought, *but he also looks so happy*.

The students enthusiastically applauded his performance, while Ben and Addie inwardly cheered Barima's success in leaving, at least momentarily, his isolated corner of the world.

It's a step forward, thought Addie.

At the end of the dance, two of the boys brought a box of fruit and vegetables to them. "Our gift and our thanks," they said.

"It's a wonderful gift," responded Addie.

"We both thank you. We'll always remember this night," said Ben.

Addie was excited about the menu for the next party.

"Ben, I think we should have American food. Do you think it would be possible to have hamburgers?"

Chuckling, Ben said, "I haven't seen a McDonald's around here, but maybe we could buy some beef or goat meat and grind it up. We could serve it like Sloppy Joes.

Addie agreed and said she would ask the bread lady to help her make the buns, and for dessert, she thought they should have chocolate chip cookies. "It's one of their favorites," she said.

On the day before the party, Addie sought out the bread lady. As she entered the large room where the bread dough was being prepared, she was awestruck at the cleanliness of the place. There was not a bit of dust or dirt anywhere. The lady had been kneading the dough on a wooden chopping block. Then she put it in a large vat, put a dish towel on it and waited for it to rise.

"Could I help form the buns?" asked Addie.

"If you're going to help, I need to see your hands," said the lady.

"I just washed them," said Addie.

"Let me see them."

Feeling like a small child, she held out her hands to the bread lady, who flung them back at her in unimpressed acceptance. Addie thought she heard some disapproving muttering, but she ignored it and started forming the buns that she placed on a large baking sheet. The dish towel was put over the dough again, and soon, the buns had risen enough to be put on large pans. Addie transported the pans to the beehive oven in the backyard. The fire, started with wood kindling, baked the buns to a golden brown. Addie was elated. After telling Ben of her experience, she asked him how he had fared.

"They killed the animal when I asked for some beef, Addie. Then they gave me a slab that they said I could pound into hamburger…which I did."

"Where is it?"

"It's in the refrigerator, cooling off. It will be fine by tomorrow…but I've had ice on my arm all afternoon." He laughed. "No, it's okay, Addie, but next time let's make it a party for vegetarians."

The party was a huge success. The students were delighted with the strange round rolls, and they loved the taste of the Sloppy Joes.

"Why do they call them Sloppy Joes?" asked one of the girls.

Why, indeed? I should have done my homework, thought Addie.

Finally she answered, "I really don't know, but if you look, you'll see that the meat mixture is loose and some of it drips down the side of the bun, so it's not neatly put together. It's…sloppy."

"And it is probably named after a man called Joe," remarked one boy as he laughed and pointed to a friend who had already spilled some of the meat mixture on his shirt. Teasing, he called, "Hello! Hello! Sloppy Joe!"

The other boys, not to be outdone, found their own targets and teased them until Addie, laughing, motioned them to stop.

But the evening was bittersweet. For the students, the tests loomed and threatened. For Addie and Ben, their time with these wonderful students in an interesting country would soon be coming to an end. Addie was worried about all of her students. Could they be ready for the test? English grammar needed strengthening; they needed more exercises in reading comprehension. They worked hard, listened carefully, and Addie was sure they prayed for success during daily meditations.

Returning from school one day, Addie was surprised to find a large pineapple on her back steps. She was wondering who had been so generous when a Nigerian lady with a small child approached her.

"You take Aretta," she said. "She is five years old and a very good little girl. Because she was born on Sunday, Aretta is her name. She can live with you and go back with you to America."

Addie looked at the child with the beautiful light brown skin, sparkling eyes, and a little crooked smile that gradually broadened and invited friendship. She was sure that Aretta was dressed in her best clothes—a long white dress with two brightly colored stripes in front and back. She twirled gracefully and ended her performance by pointing to the colorful Nigerian flag flying over the house.

She probably is intelligent too, thought Addie as she watched her display the color relationship.

Addie wondered *what was wrong. How could the mother possibly part with this child?*

"I have four other daughters," the woman continued. "We cannot feed them all. Please take her. She is such a nice little girl, and I know you would be good to her."

"I can't decide right now," Addie said gently. "It's such an important decision. We'll talk later, but you need to take her home today."

Aretta and her mother returned the next afternoon. Aretta, smiling, walked over to Addie and held out her arms. Addie lifted her onto her lap and the child snuggled contentedly.

"She likes you," said her mother. "You take her to America and give her a good life?"

"I can't promise you anything," answered Addie. "I just can't promise."

The following day, Aretta came alone. "Where's your mama?" asked Addie.

Aretta shrugged her shoulders, giggled a little, and began to dance. When she finished, Addie swept her into her arms and said gently, "You must not come here without your mother. Do you understand?"

Aretta slid out of her arms and ran to her mother who had appeared, seemingly, out of nowhere.

"You please take her?" pleaded the woman.

"I don't know," responded Addie weakly. "I just don't know."

One afternoon, she returned from market to find Aretta dancing for Ben. "Where is her mother?" asked an alarmed Addie.

"She left," answered Ben. "I know where she lives, so I told her I'd bring Aretta home."

Addie laughed as she watched Ben take the child's tiny hand and try to adjust his pace to her small steps. Finally, he lifted her in his arms and carried her.

The next day, Addie found a large yam on the back stairs. Soon another lady with a little girl appeared.

"I'm sorry," said Addie, softly, "but I can't take your daughter with me. It's just not possible."

She saw the sadness on the woman's face. "I really wish I could help you," Addie told her. "I regret that I can't. She is a lovely little child."

The woman smiled weakly and left with her little girl.

Others appeared on following days, but Addie's heart remained with Aretta. Every night, she talked to Ben about this beautiful child who she was already missing. One night, she apprehensively brought up the subject of adoption.

"I don't know if we should even entertain the thought, Ben, but when I hold her on my lap I feel that maybe this is what I was put on earth for."

Ben surprised her by saying he understood and felt the same way about the little boy in Lagos, who stood at the end behind the fence. He had gone to see him a few times when Obasi and he were in Lagos, and he talked to the children's supervisor. He was told that the boy's name was Tobi; he is three years old and both of his parents were killed in a plane crash. His father was a scientist and his mother a nurse. And both of them had gone to a Christian school like the one you are in now.

Addie looked at her husband in amazement. What was he thinking? As he talked about Tobi, she wondered if it were possible that they both wanted to love these children and give them a home.

"Could we adopt them?"

Ben was silent. Addie waited for the response that didn't come. "What do you think?" she asked again.

After heaving a big sigh, he stood and paced the floor. Addie was surprised to hear him finally say, "I don't think it's a good idea."

"Why not?"

"How many families of their race live in Roseland, Addie?"

"None, but that doesn't mean they can't."

"But the fact remains that there are none. Aretta and Tobi would be the only ones. They would feel different and out of place. Is that what we want?"

Addie's voice heightened. "No, but they would be with us, and we could help them deal with that aspect of their lives. Over here, they may starve. Tobi will be calling, 'Papa' to anyone who will listen. Can you live with that? Who will take him? What kind of home will he have? Ben, I can't believe I'm hearing you."

"I'm not a monster, Addie. I just feel that there may be other ways to help Aretta and Tobi, ways that they can stay with their own people and not suffer discrimination. That's all I am saying."

Addie looked at him in disbelief as she left the house, slamming the door. Outside, she was met by the grey parrot saying, "Hello. Hello."

"Muzzle it," she called to the bird as she began a brisk walk to calm her nerves.

Tensions were still high as Ben and Addie met for supper. Addie ate in the living room while she corrected papers. Ben ate a light supper in the kitchen while he read the *New York Times*. Encounters were polite and impersonal.

When Addie arrived from school the next day, she found a note from Ben. "Obasi and I are off to Lagos."

Addie always worried about him when he took off with Obasi. The brush was thick, and Obasi hadn't been soloing very long. What if the plane should go down? Her last conversation with Ben had been so cold and stilted and she would never be able to forgive herself for her actions if something happened to Ben.

The afternoon was long and nervous. It was 5:00 p.m. before she heard their voices. Soon Obasi left, but Ben was still outside talking to the gray parrot. She ran out to embrace him, repeating, "I'm sorry!" as he comforted her and led her into the house.

"I've been doing a lot of thinking, Addie, about Aretta and Tobi," said Ben. "I guess I hesitated because I didn't want our kids feeling they didn't belong because of the color of their skin. But then I thought about the fact that you have experienced the discrimination in Selma and Lowndes County, so if you think we can be a family in Roseland, let's go for it. If we're careful, we can make my salary stretch to include two more."

"They will need all of my attention for these first years, then when the children are both in school. I can go back to teaching," she said.

"Then I guess the case is closed," said Ben. "The defense and prosecution are in agreement on all counts."

"And I love the prosecutor—or the defendant—or whatever you were." Addie laughed.

Surprised, Addie listened as Ben told her that out of curiosity he had looked into adoption terms and found that if the leader of the tribe is in favor of adoption, it can usually proceed.

"Then we'll contact the leaders as soon as possible," said Addie, clapping her hands in excitement.

"I can contact the one in Lagos," said Ben, "but Obasi told me that the one here is gone. We may have to wait until he comes back unless there is another alternative."

"Ben," she continued, "I know we'll have some problems, but I couldn't be happier. I've been feeling guilty all along having our honeymoon while I'm working in a strange land, but maybe there is a reason…"

He silenced her with a kiss before saying, "I think we are where we should be right now. We'll have time for other places later. We have our whole lives!"

On the day before the testing was to begin, Addie received a call at school from Ben. His voice was troubled.

"I wish I didn't have to bring you this news," he said, "but Verona called and said your dad is in the hospital. He had a stroke, and they feel you might want to come home. They aren't sure about the prognosis. I'll do everything I can to help you get back home as soon as possible, if that is your decision."

Addie's hands shook as she put the phone down. *What if he dies before I get a chance to see him again?* she worried. *I'm the only one he has and I'm sitting here on the other side of the world. God, keep him alive! Please, God,* she pleaded.

Regaining some measure of control, she said goodbye to her class and arranged for Mr. Abiola to conduct the tests. Obasi waited for her at the house to fly her to Lagos and catch the afternoon flight home.

"Ben, what about the children?"

"I'll bring them as soon as I can, Addie. I don't think the adoption process will take long, and then we'll be on our way home. Don't worry about us. Just get to your father as soon as you can."

"I love you so much, Addie," he said holding her close. "We'll face whatever comes our way together."

Verona and Joe met her in Minneapolis. "I'm so sorry," Verona said, embracing her.

"How is he?"

"He has a chance, but it could go either way. He needs you, Addie. He keeps calling your name."

As they drove to Whitford, Addie gazed at the ripe fields of grain and the trees that dipped and swayed in welcome, but today, the peacefulness that she usually felt was replaced by a sense of urgency.

Walking down the hospital corridor, she felt the sweetness of memories of her father, the rides with him to town, his lessons on horseback riding, his help with training Oscar, and his quiet support through childhood, adolescence, and even adulthood. Now, it was her turn.

Thor was sleeping when she entered the room, so she sat at the foot of his bed until he awakened. As he tried to speak, it was slow, but it was there. She breathed a sigh of relief.

"Don't talk, Dad. Why don't you let me do the talking until you get stronger and it's easier for you?"

She spoke a little about her experiences in Nigeria, about the students and the soon-to-be grandchildren. He smiled and reached for her hand, holding it until he dropped off to sleep.

During the next few days, he showed some improvement. "I think he may have turned the corner," said Dr. Zomak. "He's becoming more stable, but he needs good care. Our hospital is crowded and he may do better in a rest home in another week or two."

"Let's try the rest home in Roseland," said Addie. "That's where my husband and I will be living."

A call came from Ben at the end of the week. "The red tape is terrible," he said. "I can't find a way to speed it up. The children could come with me now, but they would have to have a visitor's visa."

"And after the visa expires?" asked a worried Addie.

"I don't know, but I'll call tomorrow, and if it is feasible, I'd really like to take them home and deal with the problems as they materialize. What do you think?"

"I want them to come home too, Ben."

As she hung up, she clung to her mother's words. "Don't be upset, Addie. The sky won't fall."

The next day, another call came from Ben. "Addie," he said, excitedly, "I have the children's visas, and I hope you can meet us in New York. We'll be at the Hotel Germaine on Tuesday at noon."

"I'll be there," she shouted. The background sounds of Aretta calling "Hello, Mama," and Tobi repeating, "Mama, Mama," made her smile even wider as she greeted them and told them she loved them.

Before leaving, Addie made arrangements for her father's transfer to the rest home at Roseland. If his improvement continued, he was scheduled to move there at the end of the week. Having visited the home often while volunteering with her church, she was familiar with the surroundings and the care offered. She had always been impressed with the service given by the nursing staff.

Feeling more at ease with his condition, Addie gave her New York phone number to both the hospital and the rest home before boarding the plane for New York.

The hotel lobby of the St. Germaine in New York was gorgeous. Chandeliers shimmered and the floors were covered with thick oriental rugs, but she felt the need for larger accommodations for the four of them.

"I'm sorry, Mrs. O'Reilly," said the clerk, checking a long list of rooms, "but we don't have any of our larger suites vacant. We do have a wedding suite that isn't occupied right now. Could you possibly use that?"

The irony of sharing a wedding suite with two precocious youngsters and her husband struck Addie like a feather tickling her nose. The more she laughed, the more powerful the feather became. The clerk smiled politely. Addie took a deep breath before apologizing to him, explaining that fatigue often tweaked silly responses from her. Now she knew how badly she needed to rest before the children arrived.

The honeymoon suite with its beautiful decor made her lonesome for Ben. She wondered how the children were acting and smiled as she thought of Aretta and Tobi vying for his attention.

After saying her prayers, she lay down on the beautiful bed but couldn't sleep. Tossing and turning, she turned on the radio and listened to soothing music. Finally she slept, only to be awakened in the middle of the night by the shrill sound of the telephone. Sitting upright in bed, worried that the call could bring bad news about her father, she lifted the receiver and heard a heavily accented voice say, "This is the airport at Lagos. We are extremely sorry to tell you that the commuter plane in which your husband and children were flying has been lost, but I want you to know that we are doing everything possible to locate it."

Addie crumpled in shock. Unable to speak, she wanted to dismiss it as an afterthought of a dream that seemed to linger into consciousness; but again the distant voice broke through asking, "Mrs. O'Reilly, are you all right?"

"Yes," she answered weakly. "I just don't know what to do. I have to think."

"Of course," answered the airport control. "I can understand the shock you must be experiencing, but you must rest assured that we will keep in touch with you and call you immediately if something develops."

"When did you lose track of the plane?" she asked, finally recovering her thought processes.

"We believe it was within the first twenty minutes of the flight, but we have now extended the search."

Terrible possibilities flitted through Addie's mind as she asked, "Do you think it crashed on land or water? Could it have landed in a jungle?" Addie shuddered at the thought of wild animals.

"Please don't conjure up scenes like that," he said. "We don't know where the plane became lost, but I hope you can take comfort in the fact that we have a good record of recovery, and we will work our hardest for you.'

"They were on their way home to America to be with me. We were just starting our lives together," she said, "and now, they may be ending before they even begin. What are their chances of survival? Can you tell me that?"

"I can't put a number on it, Mrs. O'Rilley, but, as I said, our records are good regarding survival rates."

The call ended as Addie graciously thanked him. She mentally resolved to book a flight to Lagos on Wednesday night if they hadn't been found.

She looked at the clock. It was 2:10 a.m. Ten minutes ago, her life had been happy, now everything was falling to pieces. As she knelt in prayer again in the beautiful but now lonely hotel room, she sobbed out her fears and cried for help. Her spirits finally calmed, and she felt like she had when she was a little girl riding to town with her father over muddy roads and potholes. "Just hold on tight, Addie," he would say. "Soon it will be all right."

Tuesday was a long day as she decided to call Lagos and other airports along the plane's route to obtain more information. She reserved her flight to Lagos for Wednesday night to use if necessary, then planned speeches she would deliver to each airport representative.

"I need your help," she would repeat over and over to port authorities on the route. "My husband and I are in the process of adopting two children, a little three-year-old boy named Tobi who has almond colored skin, brown eyes, and black curly hair, and a five-year-old girl named Aretta, who has light brown skin and long dark hair.

"Aretta is very affectionate with everyone, and Tobi is a papa's boy who will tell you wonderful things about my husband who is six feet tall with brown hair and hazel eyes. To Tobi, he is Papa. I know you can recognize the plane, but I also need you to recognize my husband, Ben, and the children, especially if they become separated."

The calls to the airports came through clearly, but the information she wanted was sketchy. At the last airport, Addie couldn't stop the torrent of questions on her mind.

"I need to know what happened," she implored. "I need more information. Can't you tell me more about the plane? Was it a new plane? And if not, how old was it, and regardless of how old it was, was it in good shape? And was the weather calm or was it stormy? And what about the pilot? Please tell me about him. Was he experienced and could he handle problems effectively, or was he new and inexperienced? Please share with me. Please let me know."

The port authority confirmed that the weather had been threatening but not bad enough to cancel flights.

"The plane was not new," he said. "It was an older plane but definitely in good shape." He emphasized the fact that all their planes were kept in good shape, that the pilots were all well trained and able to deal well with problems on either land or water.

A long static pause raised Addie's frustration level. "Please don't hang up on me," she pleaded. "Please, please don't hang up on me."

"No, I won't," the port authority said as the static lessened, "but I have to leave you for a moment to check on a water rescue that has just taken place."

Quickly Addie asked, "Could you tell me if there were any children on that plane and were they with their father?"

As sudden static again enveloped the airways, Addie screamed again, "Please don't hang up on me! It could be my husband and Tobi and Aretta on that plane."

"Mrs. O'Reilly," he said, as the static lessened, "the passengers have not, as yet, been identified, but we will have that information shortly, at which time I shall call you immediately. In the meantime, I suggest you try to rest. Ordeals like this are very painful."

It may be painful, she thought, *but it also is giving me some hope that they are safe.*

With the conversation over, she leaned back on the couch and closed her eyes, imploring God to bring them all home and help them proceed with their lives.

"I'll do anything you want," she bargained, "if you will just bring them home."

Leaving the uncomfortable couch for the hotel bed, she dozed into sleep visualizing Ben trying to hold both Tobi and Aretta above water. She began to scream when she saw Ben lose his grip on the children and become immersed in a large tidal wave, but the shrill sound of the telephone soon brought her back to reality.

Grabbing the receiver, she quickly answered the call and heard the voice of the controller.

"Mrs. O'Reilly," he said, "the family on the plane was rescued and is doing very well, but I have the difficult task of reporting to you that it was not your family. We will, of course, keep looking for them."

Tears came as the sky continued to fall.

Wednesday morning, another long period of waiting, was more than Addie thought she could bear. She paced back and forth, looking out the window at New York's impenetrable skyscrapers. She walked down to the lobby and through the hotel shops. Usually, she loved to look in any store that sold clothing or accessories, but today, it all looked flat, devoid of any shimmer or appeal.

Finally, she took a seat in the lobby near the fireplace and watched the flickering flames. She bought a lemon Danish and began to eat it as she opened a book of poetry she had brought with her. Poems by Robert Frost always seemed to give her a sense of peacefulness, but today, her thoughts were muddled. Today, past and future roads all converged and were threatened by roadblocks.

Her thoughts were interrupted by a clap of thunder announcing an impending rainstorm. She wrapped what was left of her Danish and began walking back to the hotel room. She stopped at the front desk for messages and, finding none, entered her suite. The rain, accompanied by intense thunder and flashes of lightning, hammered against the windowpanes.

Lying down, she buried her head in a soft pillow to shut out the world.

A few minutes later, the phone rang. It was Verona calling to say her father had had a bad night, and she was worried about him. Addie began to experience cold sweats. Her shoulders ached, and her eyes were glazed from tension and lack of sleep. How could she decide what to do when her father could be dying and the rest of her family was lost? She prayed again for word from Lagos, but it didn't come. Early in the afternoon, Verona called again to tell her that her father was a little better, but his condition was not yet regarded as stable.

"Go to Lagos," said Verona. "I'll stay with your father. If there is a change, I'll move heaven and earth to contact you, but leave tonight, Addie."

She hung up the receiver and sat motionless, too tired to think or respond. Finally, she lay down and tried to rest, but her tense body could not relax. The possibility of losing her entire family crowded her thoughts, and she struggled against letting its focus paralyze her. She prayed for the strength, which her mother often spoke.

Toward evening, she called a cab to take her to the airport where she would leave for Lagos. The cab was late. She had waited thirty minutes and was afraid she would miss the plane. The last group was boarding when she arrived at the ticket window, but just before boarding, she heard her name called through the loudspeaker.

"There's a call for me," she told the attendant.

"We'll be taking off," he warned.

"No, you won't," she said authoritatively. "Your plane will wait until my call comes through." Embarrassed by her outburst, she implored, "Please wait. I need you to wait."

The attendant guided her to a phone at a desk. The call was not from the airport controller; it was from Obasi.

"No need to come back, Mrs. O'Reilly."

Addie's heart sank. They were dead. This is what she had feared would happen, what she had prayed would not end this way. "God, don't you listen?" she sobbed. Resuming her conversation with Obasi, she shouted, "Of course I'm coming back, Obasi. Do you think I would desert them, dead or alive? You can't tell…" In desperation she placed the phone's receiver on the upper part of the desk, put her head down, and cradled it in her arms, not wanting the terrible news to continue. Her shoulders rose up and down with her sobs. The attendant tried to gently lift her head, saying, "The party on the phone is still calling your name, Mrs. O'Reilly. I think you should listen."

"No, I can't," she sobbed.

The attendant put the receiver close to her ear, and she heard Obasi calling, "Mrs. O'Reilly. Mrs. O'Reilly. Don't put the phone down. I've been trying to tell you that they're not dead. They're alive!"

Obasi's words penetrated but did not seem to reach her until the attendant joined Obasi in repeating, "They're alive, Mrs. O'Reilly. They are not dead, but ALIVE!"

"Obasi," she sobbed, slowly raising her head. "Did I hear you right? Did you say—"

"Yes," he responded. "My father and I joined the search, and we found them."

"And are you all right, Obasi?"

"Yes, I'm fine."

"And Ben and the children?" she asked quickly.

"The children are doing fine, too. Ben has a broken leg and is in a wheelchair, but he is doing well."

Searching for words of thanks, Addie could only find, "I'm so grateful. How can I thank you?"

Now, emotion was in Obasi's voice as he said, "Ben is my good friend who taught me a lot." His voice broke as he continued, "It was so good to find him and the children."

"How did you do it?" asked Addie.

"I thought I saw something caught in the high brush. As we went lower, I saw it was white, and then I saw some colored stripes. It was strange, Mrs. O'Reilly, but I thought of Aretta's dress, and then we saw the plane close by. Soon the helicopter came and took them to the hospital in Lagos."

"Obasi," she said, "you're a sparrow who soared like an eagle."

"What?" asked Obasi, sounding completely baffled.

She laughed, "I'll explain when I see you. You must come to see us in America."

As she hung up the receiver, the attendant asked quietly, "Can we take off now?"

"Yes," she answered. "Yes, of course." She kept murmuring her thanks as he smiled and left.

Returning to the hotel, she found that Ben had already sent her a message, saying they were in a hospital at Lagos. He had left the hospital number, which she dialed immediately and heard his tired voice.

"We're all right, Addie," he said. "And I'm much better now that I can hear the sound of your voice. After the crash I wasn't sure it could happen."

Addie was silent. She had trouble believing the miracle of actually hearing him again. Finally, she found words to reply, "I was so scared and worried, Ben. I've missed you so much." With forced bravado, she added, "I'll never let you out of my sight again."

He smiled. "Then I'll see you Saturday night," he said. "They want to keep us for a couple days to be sure we're all right to travel."

"The honeymoon suite is waiting for us."

"What?"

"I've been in the honeymoon suite all by myself."

Ben laughingly replied, "You won't be alone for long. I love you, Addie, and here are the children. They're pulling the cord, wanting to talk to you."

Their bubbly voices were excited. Aretta, however, cried a little because she had lost her favorite dress in the brush.

"Don't worry, sweetie," comforted Addie. "We'll find one just like it when you come home."

Addie greeted the next morning with excitement. Verona had called earlier with news that her father was recovering, and now, she knew her husband and children were safe and were coming home. *I'll have a family soon*, she thought. She began to sing a familiar hymn that promised life and hope, and she smiled as she thought of Obasi and of the great gift he and his father had given her family. She would ask Obasi to come to America to continue his education. They had asked him before, but they would keep asking and inviting him to stay with them while he pursued a medical degree.

Riding a happiness cloud, she decided to go downstairs for a snack. Everything seemed brighter. Even the deep orange flames of the fireplace seemed to reach new heights in beauty and movement. She greeted strangers with such warmth that it caused them to look at her more closely to see if she were someone they knew and should embrace. She felt the happiness of Scrooge discovering the meaning of Christmas and of Dorothy finding her way home to Kansas and Aunt Em.

When Saturday finally arrived, Addie couldn't contain her excitement as she thought of seeing her family again. Her thoughts were interrupted by a phone call from the hotel clerk. "Mrs. O'Reilly, your cab is waiting," he said. Happily, she rushed to the cab that would take her to the airport to reunite with her family.

Driving in New York reminded her of traffic in Lagos. Honking horns and cars weaving in and out brought her thoughts back to the strange land from which she had left so hurriedly.

Once in the terminal, she began to relax. She was in the right direction to meet Ben and the children, but a minute seemed much more than sixty seconds. And when five long minutes had passed with no sign of them, she began to feel uncomfortable. Her annoyed feelings were suddenly interrupted by someone calling her name. Looking back, she was surprised to see Jimmy Lake, her former Roseland student who had starred as the ghost with jingle bells, waving to her. Determined to catch up with her, he was elbowing a few of the people as he tried to sprint ahead.

"Miss Carlson," he said excitedly as he caught up with her. "I thought it was you, but I wasn't sure. Oops, I heard that you married Ben O'Reilly, so I should have said 'Mrs. O'Reilly.'"

"That's all right. It's hard for me to get used to it myself. It's great to see you again, Jimmy. What are you doing in New York?"

"I'm going to drama school and working part time at a restaurant here."

Excitedly Addie cried, "I'm so proud of you, Jimmy."

Smiling shyly, he responded, "I remember how you mobilized us into action to supply books for a library in Alabama—and I still remember how you always said that a sparrow who tried hard could soar like an eagle."

Giving her a hug, he said, "I have to go now because I can't be late, but I wanted to thank you because without your help I'd still be just a 'class clown' without any serious goals."

Addie's eyes were moist as she watched him walk away, then turn around and say, "I'll always remember you, Mrs. O'Reilly."

A few minutes more passed with no sign of Ben and the children. Finally, off in the distance, she noticed a wheelchair, and as it came closer, she cheered silently for it was Ben's. He was wheeled by a flight attendant, but his body leaned forward as if to reach her sooner while she inched her way through a crowd she felt was moving extremely slow. Emotionally spent, she reached his outstretched arms, bent down, and welcomed him home.

"I love you so much, Ben," she said. "And I've been so worried that I would never see you again. Please tell me this is real, not just another dream I will wake up from and find you gone again. I couldn't stand another separation because I couldn't stand losing you and the children again—but where are they, Ben?" she asked, quickly standing and trying to locate them. "Where are the children?"

"They're back of us a little with their escort, but they'll soon catch up," said the flight attendant. Laughing, he said, "They took a quick trip to a candy shop they were passing, and each bought suckers like the ones they were given at the hospital."

He helped move both of them away from the crowd, wished them luck, then left.

Ben looked so tired, Addie thought, as his large frame struggled to find comfort in the confinement of a wheelchair that also housed a leg cast. As she embraced him again, his tired eyes told her he needed a good night's rest and a clean-cut Burma Shave. It was so good to feel his arms around her again. She wanted it to continue, but heard Aretta and Tobi shouting "Mama! Mama!"

Her heart cried when she saw little Tobi with a large bandage on his nose running toward her with outstretched arms. Aretta tried to match his pace but couldn't because of an ankle injury.

Addie swooped them both into her arms, gently pushing her fingers through Tobi's curls and stroking Aretta's locks. Comforting them, she looked at each bruise and assured them they would soon be well.

The entourage moved slowly toward the luggage area, stopping along the way only to appease the children who were entranced by the glitter of many shops and restaurants in the terminal.

Aretta smiled as she pointed to her new rose-colored dress and matching purse, then to Tobi's new blue shorts and striped shirt.

A tired Tobi grabbed at Addie's hands, crying for attention. Lifting him, she whispered, "It's all right, Tobi. We'll call a cab and soon we'll be back at the hotel, and tomorrow, we can start for home."

As they taxied to the hotel, Ben talked about their ordeal. He said that with an experienced pilot at the controls they had gone down shortly before reaching Lagos. They still don't know what caused the crash, but the pilot landed the plane skillfully and the passengers suffered only slight injuries.

"I had my carry-on with me because Aretta wanted some gum," continued Ben. "It had food in it too, so we rationed it to all the passengers because we didn't know how long we would be there. There were two other passengers."

"Did you have your knife along?"

"Yes, I did and I think it saved us."

"Really? How did you use it?"

He described how he cut some branches partway down the middle, inserted other branches and tied them together with cloth strips. When he found a slight opening in the brush, he took the branches containing Aretta's dress, climbed a tree, and threw the dress as far as he could, hoping it would land on top of the tallest brush and be seen. Then he repeated the process, using his own light shirt and other material from the passengers.

That must be when he broke his leg, thought Addie.

He laughed and continued, "I call it 'my brush with a miracle' because Obasi saw the dress. It's amazing that he could see it and recognize it."

"The experience must have been a terrible ordeal," said Addie.

"We all prayed," he said quietly, "the two Moslem passengers, the children, and me, and God answered us all."

"You're right, Ben," said Addie, smiling at him and comforting the children who were noisily tired. "He loves us equally and blesses us all."

Turning back to Ben, she added, "Do you think the four of us can hold up the sky?"

As usual, he smiled and answered, "One does what one can."

Putting his arm around her, he added, "Addie O'Reilly, I think we can soar like eagles."

ACKNOWLEDGMENTS

I wish to express my sincere gratitude to:

1. Angela Foster for her help and guidance
2. Barbara Fischer and Joni and Chris Wasberg for their suggestions and assistance
3. LaVaye Herness for typing the manuscript
4. All others who assisted in so many ways with their help and encouragement

ABOUT THE AUTHOR

Bernice Roysland, author of *Gospel of the Sparrow*, taught music in the Fergus Falls, Minnesota, public schools for thirty-five years, and English at other schools for nine years. Now, at the age of ninety-three, she is publishing her first novel.

Ms. Roysland has often linked history with her writing, including an operetta for children entitled *Susan B.*, based on the life of Susan B. Anthony.

She has also written and published *Nourishment for Body and Soul*, a book of poetry that describes the lives of earlier settlers and includes favorite recipes, both past and present.